REACH ME

(A Katie Winter FBI Suspense Thriller —Book 2)

Molly Black

Molly Black

Bestselling author Molly Black is author of the MAYA GRAY FBI suspense thriller series, comprising nine books (and counting); the RYLIE WOLF FBI suspense thriller series, comprising six books (and counting); of the TAYLOR SAGE FBI suspense thriller series, comprising three books (and counting); and of the KATIE WINTER FBI suspense thriller series, comprising six books (and counting).

An avid reader and lifelong fan of the mystery and thriller genres, Molly loves to hear from you, so please feel free to visit www.mollyblackauthor.com to learn more and stay in touch.

Copyright © 2022 by Molly Black. All rights reserved. Except as permitted under the U.S. Copyright Act of 1976, no part of this publication may be reproduced, distributed or transmitted in any form or by any means, or stored in a database or retrieval system, without the prior permission of the author. This ebook is licensed for your personal enjoyment only. This ebook may not be re-sold or given away to other people. If you would like to share this book with another person, please purchase an additional copy for each recipient. If you're reading this book and did not purchase it, or it was not purchased for your use only, then please return it and purchase your own copy. Thank you for respecting the hard work of this author. This is a work of fiction. Names, characters, businesses, organizations, places, events, and incidents either are the product of the author's imagination or are used fictionally. Any resemblance to actual persons, living or dead, is entirely coincidental. Jacket image Copyright kdshutterman, used under license from Shutterstock.com.
ISBN: 978-1-0943-9436-7

BOOKS BY MOLLY BLACK

MAYA GRAY MYSTERY SERIES
GIRL ONE: MURDER (Book #1)
GIRL TWO: TAKEN (Book #2)
GIRL THREE: TRAPPED (Book #3)
GIRL FOUR: LURED (Book #4)
GIRL FIVE: BOUND (Book #5)
GIRL SIX: FORSAKEN (Book #6)
GIRL SEVEN: CRAVED (Book #7)
GIRL EIGHT: HUNTED (Book #8)
GIRL NINE: GONE (Book #9)

RYLIE WOLF FBI SUSPENSE THRILLER
FOUND YOU (Book #1)
CAUGHT YOU (Book #2)
SEE YOU (Book #3)
WANT YOU (Book #4)
TAKE YOU (Book #5)
DARE YOU (Book #6)

TAYLOR SAGE FBI SUSPENSE THRILLER
DON'T LOOK (Book #1)
DON'T BREATHE (Book #2)
DON'T RUN (Book #3)

KATIE WINTER FBI SUSPENSE THRILLER
SAVE ME (Book #1)
REACH ME (Book #2)
HIDE ME (Book #3)
BELIEVE ME (Book #4)
HELP ME (Book #5)
FORGET ME (Book #6)

PROLOGUE

On this icy morning, Henry White had been given the most dangerous job of his career so far. Striding along the prison corridor, he checked the handcuffs and stun gun were in place on his belt. He felt nervous, hoping the inmate transfer would go without a hitch.

"Don't worry," Joe, his colleague, reassured him as he walked alongside. "This guy's been in solitary for months. He'll come quietly. They always do. They're just glad to get back to a normal cell."

But Henry still felt uneasy. After all, this prisoner had spent three months in solitary because he'd killed a fellow inmate. And that was after the string of murders he'd committed outside, before finally being arrested.

Carl Dolan was a violent, brutal serial killer. The most dangerous type of murderer there was. But Henry had to get used to this part of his job, now that he was on a higher pay grade and working in the maximum-security section of this northerly New York state prison.

They reached the steel door that separated this solitary confinement area from the rest of the prison. Joe took the bunch of keys off his belt and unlocked the door. It clanged loudly as he opened it.

The two men stepped through it and headed down the short corridor to the solitary confinement cell.

As he approached, staring curiously through the thick, steel-barred door, Henry was shocked by how small the windowless cell was. It wasn't much larger than an elevator: a concrete box, with a concrete bed, and a thin mattress. There were a few rough, gray blankets, and a small ventilation grille high up near the ceiling. The steel sink and toilet, within arm's reach of the bed, looked dull and dirty. The walls were blank, decorated only by scuffs and stains.

Henry couldn't imagine spending twenty-three hours a day in this space, with no human contact apart from the occasional passing guard.

The prisoner sat on the bed. He had his elbows on his knees and his chin was resting on his hands. He looked up as they arrived.

Henry blinked. He'd thought Dolan would be a big man, with a lot of muscle. But under his gray prisoner's outfit, he looked rather skinny.

He was average height, lean and wiry. That reassured Henry. If he caused trouble, he and Joe could easily contain him.

"Carl Dolan," Joe said. "We're here to take you back to the cells. Put your hands through the gap. We're going to cuff you and shackle you."

Henry's hands were shaking slightly as he took the bunch of keys and unlocked the handcuffs and the leg irons, handing the irons and the cuffs to Joe. He had to concentrate hard to stop showing his nerves. He didn't want to give Dolan any idea that he was unsure. And he saw Dolan was watching him. His eyes were a very light, glacial blue.

"Cuff me and shackle me? What for?" Dolan asked. His voice was surprisingly soft.

"For your own protection," Joe replied automatically. "For the walk back to the general prison population."

"I'm going back there?"

"That's right. Your solitary term ended today."

Dolan shook his head. "I don't want to go. Those guys are going to kill me." He looked pale and scared as he spoke.

Joe glanced at Henry as if to say: See? He's broken.

Dolan put his hands through the gap. His fingernails were uneven and had been roughly trimmed. Then Joe stepped forward and briskly snapped the handcuffs shut. He locked them to the steel loop on the slot before moving to the cell door.

Joe unlocked it while Henry stood watching. Then Joe moved inside and, working carefully, shackled Dolan's ankles. Henry felt a sense of relief when their prisoner was fully restrained.

When the shackles were in place, Joe took hold of Dolan's arm.

"Check the cell?" he asked Henry.

Carefully, Henry moved through the cell, checking that everything was in place and that Dolan hadn't managed to break any part of the cell's fittings or fixtures to make a weapon. The cell was so small and bare it only took a minute to search.

"All fine," he said.

"Let's go."

Henry walked outside the cell. He undid the lock that secured the handcuffs to the iron loop. Then he headed back into the cell. With the prisoner in cuffs and shackles, all that remained was the five-minute walk through the chilly corridors. Now that this part of the transfer was done, he didn't know why he'd been nervous at all. Joe was right. It was easy. Coming out of solitary, the inmates didn't want to make trouble.

Joe grasped Dolan's arm firmly. He was whistling under his breath as he turned the skinny man in the direction of the door.

And then, in front of Henry's horrified eyes, Dolan suddenly convulsed. He doubled over, screaming.

"What the hell?" Henry rushed back inside the cell. Joe still had hold of Dolan's arm. He was tugging at it, trying to keep the prisoner on his feet.

"What is it, man? What's happened?" Joe shouted, leaning forward in concern.

And, as he did that, Dolan struck.

With a twist of his arms, he trapped Joe's neck in the circle of his cuffed hands. Joe had time to give one loud, astonished yell. Then he choked, a terrible, retching sound.

Gasping, Joe staggered toward the cell door, desperately trying to get away. He jerked his arm to one side, trying to throw off his assailant. But Dolan was holding on tightly, his hands like pincers around his neck. Joe's eyes were wide with terror.

Dolan twisted his arms, pressing them on either side of Joe's head.

"Argh!" Joe started to collapse onto the floor. His body was limp and at the same time his face twisted in agony. And then, Henry heard a dull, snapping noise and Joe crumpled to the floor.

The situation had turned lethal. In a moment, it had become Henry's worst nightmare. He grabbed the stun gun from his belt, his hands shaking badly now. He needed to take him down, immediately.

He turned on the stun gun and lunged toward Dolan, but somehow, the man was ready for him. He whipped his upper body forward and head-butted Henry directly in the face with his forehead.

Henry felt a blinding pain. His nose crackled with the impact. His eyes streamed as he staggered down to his knees. Choking on blood, he gasped for air.

"Help! Help!" Even as Henry sputtered the words, coughing blood away, he realized how futile they were, because this was solitary confinement. The gate to this section was a hundred yards down and far out of earshot. That was the point of solitary. Nobody could hear your screams.

Henry scrambled to his feet. Joe was on the floor, lying on his side. His head was twisted to one side. A thin trickle of blood seeped across the concrete.

He kept scrambling unsteadily to his feet, desperately trying to get the stun gun into place for a second attempt, but Dolan was too quick for him.

Using both his cuffed hands like a battering ram, he punched Henry in the stomach. The blow knocked him off his feet.

He hit the floor hard, and felt the wind rush out of him. The stun gun flew out of his hand and clattered against the wall. The keys on his belt jangled with the impact.

Then Dolan was on top of him. He grabbed Henry's throat with his hands. He pressed down, and Henry felt the cold metal choking him. Henry tried to fight back, but Dolan was too strong. He felt his airway closing as Dolan's thumb pressed against his Adam's apple. He tried to pull free, but Dolan had him in a vise.

A killing machine, Henry remembered. That's what the guards had called this man and now he knew why.

"Sorry, man," Henry heard Dolan say, almost regretfully. His voice sounded far away. "I got things to do. Places to go."

His eyes were like blue icebergs, Henry thought, trapped on the floor, unable to move as darkness swallowed him.

CHAPTER ONE

Katie Winter thrust her paddle into the raging, ice-cold waters. Turning, she grinned at her sixteen-year-old twin.

"Got the rapids ahead, Josie. But the river's high. We should miss the rocks. You ready?"

Grinning back, pushing her dark brown hair back from her face, Josie nodded. Her green eyes sparkled.

Cold water splashed around Katie, icing her skin, but she barely noticed. She felt warmed by the adrenaline rush of doing something dangerous. Forbidden, in fact, because her father refused to let them go out in their kayaks when the river was so wild.

Even Josie hadn't wanted to go out that morning, but Katie had persuaded her.

The whitewater was going fast and furious, as if it were alive. The river crashed and frothed, rising up in waves.

Shaking her wet hair back from her face, Katie gazed ahead.

"Yep, we'll go through those rapids. It'll be our best ride yet," she said.

"We will!" Josie sounded excited. "Race you?"

"Sure."

The rapids were like a roller coaster, Katie thought, a roller coaster with no rails and no seatbelt. All you could do was hold on to your paddle and hope to survive.

But Katie wasn't worried. She and Josie had kayaked all their lives. They knew what they were doing. And they had each other.

"Ready?" Katie asked.

"Ready!"

They plunged forward, digging their paddles into the water. Josie was faster. Her kayak surged ahead, her life jacket bright against the frothing water.

Katie felt the spray hit her, splashing up into her face and eyes. She blinked hard, trying to see where the river was taking her. On either side of her she saw the banks, wild and green with late summer growth. High above her head stretched the flat, gray sky.

And then, they were into the rapids.

But they were rougher than she'd expected. So much worse than she'd thought they would be. Katie felt the river snatch at her. It had a personality of its own, and she realized that she'd misjudged the power and force of it.

Above the roar of the rapids, she heard Josie scream. "Katie!" The waves were so high and rough she couldn't see her twin any longer.

Gritting her teeth, she dug her paddle in again. The kayak surged forward, veering past the dangerous rocks with inches to spare.

"Katie!" Josie's cry came from behind her, and Katie glanced round, glimpsing her twin. With a surge of panic, she saw Josie was having trouble now, her kayak fighting the current. She was heading straight for a rock.

"Go left! Go left!" Katie screamed. The next set of rapids was already looming. The river rushed around her, a roaring, thundering wall of water. She saw the boulders, dark shapes under the churning waves. She knew she couldn't stop. She couldn't turn.

"Josie!" she yelled, risking another glance back.

She saw her sister's kayak tip up sideways. Josie disappeared under the water.

"No!"

The impossible, a catastrophe, had happened, and she couldn't help her.

All she could do was fight the raging water, trying to get to the other side of the rapids without losing control. She couldn't see a thing over the floods. But she knew her twin was lost.

"No!" Katie screamed again.

And then, finally, she fought her way out of the dream and her eyes flew open.

Reality filtered back. She was in her airplane seat, cold air rushing down onto her, cooling the sweat on her forehead. The passenger next to her was staring at her curiously, with some concern.

"You okay? Should I call a stewardess?" the elderly man asked.

"Sorry," Katie muttered. "Bad dream. I'll be fine."

She took a deep breath, trying to shake off the chilling remnants of the recurring nightmare. She wasn't in the kayak. She was on a plane, heading north, going to start a new phase of her career as the FBI representative in the special cross-border task force fighting crime in the Upper Peninsula area.

At that moment, Katie felt ill-prepared for her new role. Her heart was still pounding in fear. She was gripping her seat's armrests just like she'd gripped onto the paddle, fighting against the river that wanted to tear it away. Slowly, she released her grasp. Forced her hands to relax.

If only it had been a dream. But it hadn't. She'd been reliving an actual memory. It was the tragedy that had defined the rest of her life. Josie had disappeared and never been found.

Now, she was heading back to the part of the world where the pain was waiting for her, as raw and intense as it had ever been. This where her memories were buried, the place all her nightmares emanated from. It was where her estranged parents still lived. That incident had destroyed her relationship with her mother and father forever.

After Katie had finally escaped the river, she'd searched everywhere for Josie, hunting along the riverbanks, calling until she was hoarse. Finally, she headed back home on cotton-wool legs, her eyes streaming with tears, shivering with cold and dread.

Her father had been furious. She'd never seen him so angry, or so mortally afraid. Quickly, a search party had been assembled, comprised of volunteers and local police. They'd combed that section of river. A few hours later, they'd found Josie's canoe, damaged, wedged in rocks a few miles down. And then they'd found the life jacket, hooked on a branch.

Katie swallowed hard. Her eyes felt hot and sore as she remembered that bright jacket, snagged on a tree, and what that sight had meant.

The police had interviewed locals, hoping someone might have seen her. Perhaps she'd been knocked on the head and suffered amnesia; perhaps she was still alive.

But there was no sign of Josie. She had vanished without a trace.

She remembered how her mother had stood in the front hall and stared at her, the anger and pain on her face filling Katie with despair.

"What do you have to say for yourself?" her mother had demanded, sobbing. "What happened out there?"

"Nothing. Nothing. We were just kayaking."

"But in that weather? You knew you shouldn't have! Now Josie is gone."

"It was an accident. We must have hit the rapids the wrong way. I don't know what could have happened to her, or how her life jacket came off, or how she disappeared."

And then, the news arrived that had broken Katie. Broken all of them. One of the men the police had found near the site where she'd disappeared was Charles Everton, an escaped prisoner and known killer.

When they asked him if he'd seen Josie, if he'd played any role in her disappearance, he had just smiled. He hadn't said a word.

Katie was convinced he'd found her. He'd taken her. She'd always promised herself that one day, somehow, she would come face to face with him again in the prison where he was serving his life sentence. She'd ask him what had happened to Josie and demand the truth from him.

The pain felt as vivid as it had done on that fateful day. She knew it would never get better, but Katie reminded herself that this experience had shaped her life. It was why she'd chosen to join the FBI and to spend her career hunting down monsters, like the one she was sure had killed her twin.

The plane was flying over Lake Huron now, its surface inky black. She stared down at the water. It looked cold and threatening. Beyond, the wintry landscape was white, snowbound and featureless.

In these vast, wild areas, people lived off the grid and often beyond the law.

She couldn't make a difference to Josie. Josie was gone. But she could make a difference to others. Her experience and local knowledge would count. She would use it in a positive way to hunt down other monsters, fugitives who were hiding out and hoping never to be found.

Glancing down at her phone with a shiver, she saw that a message had just come in from Scott, the task force leader.

"I've just been notified a prisoner has escaped from a New York jail. If they don't recapture him and he tries to flee north, he's in our territory and the task force can get involved. I've asked for more information asap. We're meeting at 10 a.m. to discuss it."

CHAPTER TWO

As she pulled up outside the small apartment in Sault Ste Marie, Katie felt more impatient about the potential new case than she did about dropping her bags off in the rental she'd be occupying. The task team had relocated to this city, set on the St Mary's River in the heart of the Great Lakes, because it was central, and straddled both the US and Canada. Her move here was the start of a whole new life.

Katie was used to traveling light. FBI agents were moved frequently, and as a serial killer specialist, she'd moved around more times than most.

She didn't have much gear. Two large bags carried the sum total of the clothes she needed to set herself up in her new location, and a couple of boxes had already been delivered to the apartment.

Climbing out of the car, she wheeled her bags inside and picked up the keys from the apartment's post box in the lobby. Then she took the elevator to the third floor. Heading to apartment 301, she opened the door.

Inside, she was pleased by the stark, utilitarian space that she saw. The place had a basic, clean look about it, with cool, dark wood floors and plain white walls.

The apartment's living room was furnished with an L-shaped sofa, a desk and lamp, a bookcase and a TV stand. The kitchen was simple, with new, almost-white counters and a modern white table and chairs. There was a small bathroom, with a shower and a basic toilet. Beyond that was her bedroom, with a double bed, a wardrobe, and a small chest of drawers.

She carried in her bags and set them by the bedroom door. Then she headed over to the window and pushed back the curtains. Even on this gloomy day, the views were spectacular, with the St Mary's River winding its way between the two countries. She was on the Michigan side and could look across the water to Canada.

Katie had discovered that this scenic town, one of the oldest French settlements in North America, had originally been established along the fur trade route. It then became a hub for the steel and forestry industries. Although the city's population had declined in recent years to around seventy thousand as these industries shrunk, it was still a popular destination for tourists and sports lovers, especially in winter.

Turning away from the compelling view, the first thing she did was check the locking mechanisms in this modern apartment. Like all FBI agents, she was always aware of security. Even though she knew that she was in a relatively safe and busy part of town, and she'd be working with an experienced law enforcement team, she had to be vigilant.

The door and window locks were all in good working order. That reassured her that Scott had chosen well.

Katie unpacked a few basics and then checked the time. It was now nine-thirty a.m. and that meant she could head to the new office, which was also on the Michigan side. Scott had told her it was a three-minute drive, or a ten-minute walk, from her apartment.

She felt surprisingly excited about seeing her team again, after the last case she'd worked on. And about seeing Detective Leblanc, who would be her investigation partner.

Deciding to walk, Katie wrapped herself in her parka and headed out. Stepping onto the street, she gazed at the town around her, taking in the sights and sounds. The downtown area was small but charming, and she noticed many of the buildings had a European feel to them. Thanks to the tourists, there was a buzz of activity, despite the frigid weather. The place was busy, with people walking, waiting at bus stops, shopping, and heading to their cars.

Ahead of her was the building Scott had given her the coordinates for. This would be their new headquarters.

Opening the door, she stepped in and looked around. Scott mentioned the building had once been a warehouse, and it still had the same spacious, industrial feel to it. But now it was also clearly a police headquarters.

The place had been equipped with half a dozen new desks, computers and chairs in place, and a couple of large whiteboards on the walls. Beyond that was a dividing wall that she guessed might lead to a makeshift meeting room.

Scott was standing by the small kitchen area in the office, and he turned as she entered.

"Great, you're here," he said, walking over to her and shaking her hand. The gray-haired detective was wearing jeans and a heavy green parka. "How was your flight? And your apartment?"

"My flight was fine. The apartment's a great choice." Katie smiled.

Beyond him, at the coffee station, she saw the tall, fit Leblanc. Instantly, she clocked his neatly trimmed dark hair and his olive skin. His dark eyes widened when he saw her. A smile spread over his face.

Not exactly a welcoming expression, she decided. This was more of a smug smile.

"I knew you would not be able to stay away," he declared in a French-accented voice that she knew was far more Paris than Quebec. Paris was, after all, where her investigation partner had spent most of his life.

"Good to see you again," she said, as he walked over to her. She shook his hand, thinking that he had not changed a bit. He was tall, dark, and well-built. And his dark eyes had a cool, assessing look to them.

He walked back to the coffee station, leaving her to follow. He was everything she remembered she liked, and everything she didn't. She had a feeling he was going to find ways to get to her in a very personal manner. Her case partner could be both invaluable, and insufferable.

"We'll start our meeting now, since we're all here," Scott said. "We'll have a general briefing and await more information on the case I mentioned to you, so that we can make a call on whether to get involved. Come through." He checked his phone, clearly impatient for the information to arrive.

Katie poured herself a coffee and headed through the doorway in the dividing wall, to the meeting room where the rest of the team was seated.

She recognized the Canadian detective Clark, and police psychologist Chris Johnson, as well as detective Damien Anderson from the Toronto Police Department. They were good people. Perceptive, diligent, talented. Together they had cracked the first case she'd been involved in, the one that had brought her here.

"Morning, gents," she greeted them, appreciating the chorus of responses. None of them were smug, she noted. Only her own partner. For a moment she wondered if she'd misjudged her ability to work with Leblanc without sparks flying off the both of them.

There was a sense of urgency in the meeting room. Katie knew everyone was waiting to hear more about the potential new case.

"First of all, some information on the way we'll be working," Scott said, checking his phone yet again as he spoke. "We've set up a feed through to the emergency rooms of all the local police precincts, as well as the area's 911 calls. That way we'll see all cases as they arrive.

We won't be in a situation where we end up getting involved three days or a week later. We've been there. Done that. There were too many deaths."

All around the table, Katie saw people nodding solemnly. Delays had cost the team heavily in the previous case. It could have been very different if they had been involved from the start.

"When we set up the feed this morning, the escaped prisoner was one of the first notifications. I called local police immediately."

At that moment, Scott's phone buzzed. Quickly, he opened it.

Katie exchanged glances with the others. An atmosphere of tension and expectancy filled the room

"We've got more details," he said.

"What are they?" Clark asked eagerly.

"His name is Carl Dolan, and he's a serial murderer who's been inside for just two years. He has committed a string of murders in the US and Canada."

Katie saw solemn nods from around the table. Clearly, the name rang a bell.

"I worked on one of his murder cases a few years ago, near Toronto. It was a vicious, brutal crime and created a massive amount of fear in the community," Clark said, his voice hard. "He's a Canadian resident, who committed murders in Canada and then moved south to New York, where he was captured after killing again. He's killed seven times to my knowledge, starting at age twenty. He's thirty now."

"He escaped during a move from solitary back to the cells," Scott continued. "He killed two prison guards and walked out using their keys and access cards. The guards tried to follow once they realized what had happened but lost him outside. There's heavy snow and strong winds there at the moment. They have no idea which direction he's fled. He could have crossed the state line to the south, possibly heading for Allegheny National Forest which would be a good place to hide out. Or he could be heading north and looking to get over the border. If it's south, we can't take it on. If it's north, we can get involved immediately."

"Where did he escape from?" Anderson asked.

"From the Northfields maximum-security jail, which is in New York state, near Ellicottville. It's nearly a hundred miles from the Canadian border."

The name hit Katie like a hammer blow. Memories surged inside her as her skin prickled in remembered fear.

Northfields was the place where Everton was serving his sentence. Her sister's suspected killer was incarcerated there.

"We have to find Dolan," she said reflexively.

She couldn't bear to think of a serial killer escaping from that prison again. Dolan had to be recaptured as soon as possible, or many more lives would be destroyed.

CHAPTER THREE

Leblanc felt surprised that Katie was so on edge as Scott took them through the basic outline of the case. She was practically jumping up and down to get involved, and they didn't even know which direction the prisoner had fled yet.

There'd be plenty more to do. The feed was updating continually. There was a lot going on that was relevant to their area, even if it wasn't the same scale as an escaped killer.

"I don't think we need to go," he argued. "The prison is far from the closest border. And it's snowing, which will slow him down."

Katie stared at him. "There's no time," she said. "We have to get involved, and we have to get to Northfields."

Leblanc looked at her more closely. There was an anxiety in her eyes that he did not understand.

"What's the status of the search?" he asked Scott. "Is there any progress?"

"Reports are coming in fast," he said, scanning the latest updates before replying. "It's in full swing, with the New York State Police already involved, and Pennsylvania standing by and monitoring the state border. And the US Marshals are on site, too. They'll be looking through the back country for him. Local police on the ground are going street by street."

"And they haven't found him yet?" Leblanc frowned. "Are you sure? In this weather, I'd think it would be impossible to hide."

"I agree with you. I don't think he'll be able to hide for long. Right now, we're just observing the situation," Scott said. "The concern is that he heads for the border."

"Why would he do that?" Anderson asked. "It would make far more sense for him to go south, as far and fast as he could. Hide out in the forest."

Katie shook her head. "He's a Canadian resident. He'll want to go back to familiar territory. If he's from this area, he knows how to survive in the wilderness in winter. He'll get dressed for the cold, and he'll head for someplace where he can lay low."

"He might not get that far," Leblanc argued. Forcing himself to lean back in his chair, he took a deep breath. He did not like being rushed like this. This was not the way to handle things. What was up with Katie, he wondered.

Katie leaned forward, her gaze fixed on the screen. "We have to stop him," she insisted.

The way she was saying it, Leblanc wondered if it meant more to her.

"What's the deal, Katie?" Leblanc said. "Tell us why this is personal to you."

Katie looked at him, surprised and, Leblanc thought, defensive. He sensed everyone in the room was now waiting for her reply.

"You know it's not personal. A dangerous killer's at large. Right now, every person who's on site and helping with this search will potentially prevent more murders."

Leblanc tilted his head as he stared at her. That was a good reply, but it sounded more like a justification for what she wanted. He didn't think she was telling the whole truth. But at least now she knew what he thought.

As he considered the implications of their international task force getting involved in a local hunt on US soil that was already in full swing, his own sense of unease grew. This could become political.

Leblanc himself had fiercely resisted the FBI's involvement in the task team because sometimes, keeping it local was better, faster, and more effective. As it turned out, Katie had been a huge asset to the investigation and the task force. But that didn't mean it was the right call now.

"I'd like to monitor the feeds for longer," he said. "We need to be more informed of the situation before we can decide whether we're best off joining or keeping out of it."

"We need to join!" Katie insisted. She glanced pleadingly at Scott. "This is a serial killer. It's my area of expertise. He presents a real danger to anyone who gets in his way."

"I hear you," Scott said. "But we have to make sure we're not overstepping our mandate."

Leblanc watched as the screen filled with data. A map of New York state appeared with the prison highlighted. The prison itself was situated in a remote area surrounded by thick forests, fields and rivers, with local roads leading into it. The weather conditions were clear in the satellite images, right down to the heavy snowfall.

"He killed his cellmate and has just killed two other men," she went on. "He won't think twice about killing again if he believes he's at risk."

Leblanc saw that she was strung so tight she was almost vibrating with tension. He looked at her and saw her eyes were wide with concern.

"You think he's going to cross the border?" Leblanc asked.

"I do," she said.

"How can you predict that?" Leblanc challenged her.

"He did whatever it took to escape from jail. He'll do whatever it takes to avoid being rearrested. And that means getting out of the country," Katie argued. Leblanc noted the stubborn jut to her chin, marring the otherwise flawless structure of her face. "There's far more space to disappear in Canada."

"One advantage he does have is that it's very cold out. There won't be many people on the roads, and it will be difficult to trace him if he stays off the main highways," Clark observed thoughtfully.

"I believe he will do that," Katie said. "A guy who manages to escape from a maximum-security prison is smart and ruthless. He'll do what he needs to, in order to survive and keep ahead of the search."

Scott nodded, and Leblanc could see he was taking in all the feedback from the various members of the task force. Tension felt heavy in the air.

"I don't think we have to go," Anderson said. "If the State Police can stop him, then that's best. We'd be wasting our time and resources. Shouldn't we study the feed further? I just saw something else come up, an armed robbery on the A15 highway north of Champlain. Two robbers shot a store owner and fled. That's right on the border, and in our jurisdiction."

"Well, why don't we get involved with both crimes, rather than ignoring the more serious one? There are enough of us," Katie suggested. As she turned to Anderson, Leblanc saw the pain and anger in her eyes. "I know Dolan's type," she said. "I have spent years hunting down people exactly like him. I know what he's capable of, and I know he's not going to stop killing."

"Surely he will want to avoid people?" Leblanc argued.

"He'll need transport, but he has no obvious means of getting hold of a car. He could steal one, but even that is a risk. No, I think he'll get someone to give him a ride. For that he'll need to approach someone and ask for help. Every interaction presents a risk."

"Katie's right," Johnson said, and Leblanc felt surprised that the psychologist on the team was coming down firmly on her side. "The killer will probably want to move fast. He'll need warmth, transport, and to arm himself. Any of those represents a risk he will kill again, although it's not guaranteed. But he has no inhibition to kill. If we want to save lives, then the more people that get involved, the better."

Leblanc saw Katie glance gratefully at Johnson.

"Alright. Thank you for your input." Scott paused thoughtfully and Leblanc knew he was assessing what each team member had said.

Finally, Scott made his call.

"I think, taking everything into account, that this man represents a danger, and that our early involvement might save lives," he said. "However, I'm not going to commit the whole team. Leblanc and Winter, you two go there. You can do an initial assessment and report back. We'll make a final call from there. The rest of the team will be assigned to the armed robbery."

Leblanc heard Katie catch her breath, a small, involuntary sound. She was staring determinedly at the screen.

"If nothing else, this will be a good opportunity for our task force to gain experience in working cooperatively with other law enforcement. So, you two get going. I'll notify all the other role players to stand by. We'll organize a chopper to fly you straight to the maximum-security prison, and I'll arrange a car for you on that side if you need it. Be ready to leave in half an hour," Scott said.

With a scrape of chairs, everyone stood up. There was an air of excitement and purpose in the room, but Leblanc didn't share it. He still felt confused by why Katie was so hell bent about taking this case on.

Leblanc resolved that he was going to watch her carefully and find out why.

CHAPTER FOUR

Two hours later, the chopper landed on the helipad outside Northfields Maximum Security Prison. Katie felt as if she'd been holding her breath for most of the ride. She couldn't believe she was here at last. Facing the place that she'd imagined in her waking hours and her nightmares, for more than ten years.

She undid her seatbelt, took off her headphones, and climbed out, waiting for Leblanc to join her. The wind was strong, the air cold and crisp. The white of the snow almost blinded her. She felt the cold strike into her bones. Despite her heavy boots and coat, she shivered as she stared at the prison.

The walls of the maximum-security prison were surrounded by twelve-foot-high fences and razor wire, electrified and equipped with motion sensors. Dozens of surveillance cameras covered every inch of the prison grounds. Anybody who tried to climb over the wall would be electrocuted instantly. If a man tried to burrow under it, he'd be crushed by the rolling gate under the fence. If he used a ladder to get over, he'd bounce off the electric fence.

Dolan had gotten out, calmly using his victims' uniforms and access cards to escape. But others were still imprisoned inside.

Katie walked up to the prison gate, with her heart thudding against her ribs. She felt as if she were being sucked down into a black hole, into a dark and terrifying place.

There were several guards at the gate, looking anxious. This escape had clearly shaken everyone and now they were on a security red alert.

"Detective Leblanc, from the cross-border task force," Leblanc introduced himself, showing his ID.

"FBI Special Agent Katie Winter." She did the same.

"I'll call the head warden," one of the guards said, while another checked their IDs carefully. He got on the phone immediately and made a short call.

"The warden is on his way," he said. "Come through."

He led the way inside the prison. The maximum-security detention center was a cold and grim place, Katie saw.

The hallways were institutional gray, lined with steel doors. The walls were painted with white enamel, but the paint was chipped and faded. The floor was made of worn linoleum.

The few doors they passed were all closed, and the air was thick with the smell of disinfectant. Katie felt nauseous.

She didn't normally get claustrophobic, but suddenly she felt that she couldn't breathe. She glanced at Leblanc, hoping he hadn't noticed. Of course, he had, and was looking at her curiously.

"Here is Smith, the head warden," the guard said, as a man walked briskly toward them.

The warden was a tall, husky man with a shaved head and a grim expression. He looked like someone who could handle the worst of trouble, but still wasn't pleased that it had landed. He wore a brown uniform, with a badge on the front. His thin face was grim, his eyes hard.

"I've heard about your task force," he said. "Welcome to Northfields. Wish the circumstances were better."

He shook hands with each of them and watched as they passed their ID badges through the scanner at the gate leading to the maximum-security section.

"What happened? How did Dolan escape?" Leblanc asked.

"I'll walk you through it," Smith said.

They followed Smith into the security control room, a gray-walled room with a bank of monitors on the wall. Two guards in uniform were watching the monitors.

"Dolan killed the two guards inside his cell. We don't know what happened as the camera footage for that area only reaches as far as the door and the corridor. Budget constraints," Smith shrugged angrily. "The guards were good men and well trained, although one of them was new to the maximum-security section. I suspect Dolan faked something, lured them in, got them out of range of the cameras and then struck."

He pointed to the monitor. "This is the last known footage of Dolan and the guards. At zero-seven-thirty, when it was still dark, Dolan is at the cell door and they're handcuffing him according to protocol. Here's your killer."

Staring up at the screen, Katie saw the man was lean, and looked average height, but it was difficult to see much else about his build. He had an angular face and short, cropped brown hair. He was wearing a prison-issue gray sweater, the sleeves rolled up, and a pair of scuffed sneakers on his feet.

"You can see the two guards at work. The one on the left has the keys," Smith said.

Katie thought she could see Dolan's eyes following those keys.

"This is our next footage. As you can see, the man who walks out looks like one of the guards, but it wasn't. It was Dolan, wearing a guard's uniform, with an access card and keys on his belt. By then, the guards were both dead, at the back of the cell. One had a broken neck; the other was strangled."

Katie shivered. Dolan walked with casual confidence. He was clearly an ice-cool operator.

"This is the final footage," Smith said, nodding at the guard.

The guard pressed a button. The screen flashed, then lit up with the same image, but in slow motion. Dolan walked out of the solitary confinement wing, walking calmly, nonthreatening. The guards were talking to each other, not paying attention to Dolan.

"Was there any sign of a struggle? Of a fight?" Katie asked.

"Nothing," Smith said. "From the scene, it was clear the guards were killed almost instantly. They didn't have time to put up a fight or escape the cell."

"Who found the bodies?" Leblanc asked.

"One of the guards in the next wing had finished his shift. On the way back, he noticed the door to that passage was unlocked. He went to investigate, and he found Dolan's cell was open. He saw the bodies, and he called for help."

So that was how he'd done it. In a bold, violent move, he'd put on the uniform of one of the guards he'd killed, used their cards, and simply strolled out of the prison with easy confidence.

Katie knew immediately this was no ordinary level of criminal they were dealing with.

"Once outside, where did he go?" she asked.

"We're trying to track down CCTV from the main entrance, but so far we've got nothing useful," Smith said. "With the wind and the snow, the cameras on the gate are also out of operation. So after he's out, the trail goes cold. No vehicles are missing, though, so wherever he went, it must have been initially on foot."

"What's the current status of the prisoners?" Leblanc asked.

"Strict lockdown. We're not taking any chances that someone else tries to copy this. I've requested extra guards to be deployed here for the next few days," Smith said.

Katie nodded. She thought that was a good call. She'd visited prisons after a breakout a few times so far and had seen what one escape did and how restless and violent the atmosphere felt. It would be a dangerous and volatile place until things settled down again.

"We should take a look at where he got out," she said. "Speak to the guards there. See what they recall."

Leblanc nodded. "We should also question some of the other inmates. He could have talked about his plans with his neighbors. The prison grapevine knows things."

"I can go and do that?" Katie suggested, guessing that she might be more persuasive to get them to open up to her.

"I don't want you going in there on your own," Leblanc replied immediately. Katie was surprised by how instant and reflexive his response was.

"Whoever goes into the cells will be accompanied by a prison guard at all times," Smith explained.

Katie nodded. "Let me go, then?"

"I'll walk with you to the exit, and you can speak to the guards there," Smith said to Leblanc. He turned to the guard. "Go with Agent Winter. All the prisoners are in their cells. Just make sure security protocols are maintained."

"Yes, sir," the guard said.

Katie looked at the screen once more. She could still see Dolan's lean, calm face, those icy, pale eyes. But it wasn't that face she was seeing in her mind. The features seemed transposed over the other face, the one she would never forget. Trauma surged inside her again. Dolan had to be caught. Had to!

"Let's go, Agent Winter," the guard said, gesturing to the door.

CHAPTER FIVE

As Katie headed into the maximum-security jail block, she could sense the unease and restlessness. She could hear shouted voices, the clang of doors.

Walking down the corridor with the guard, she felt eyes were following her, watching her. There was tension in the air, a restless energy. She could feel the weight of malevolence that she was out, and they were in. It was like a physical force, pressing against her.

A narrow cell door opened, and an inmate stood in the steel-barred gap.

"Hey, can you get me some cigarettes?" he shouted at the guard.

"This is Dolan's neighbor," the guard muttered. "Dolan was in the cell next door."

Katie turned to him. The man stared back at her, his lips pressed together. He looked her up and down, and as he did, his cellmate strode to the door, looking aggressive.

"What you want with us?"

"I want to ask you about Dolan."

"We don't know about that," the inmate muttered, turning his back.

Katie stayed calm. She'd had plenty of experience with people who'd treated her with less respect.

"Why do you want to know?" the inmate who'd asked for cigarettes said, sounding suspicious.

"He escaped. He must have had plans. I need to know where he went."

"I don't know. We stayed away from him. He wasn't a nice guy. He only spoke to his cellmate."

"He said nothing to you?" Katie asked, feeling troubled.

"The one time, I got in his way during exercise without meaning to. He came up to me later and told me he'd make me pay. That nobody messes with him. It sounded more like a promise than a threat," the inmate said. "I kept far away from him after that."

"Did he have any friends in the prison?" Katie asked.

The inmate shrugged. "He didn't have any friends. He was very violent and dangerous. One of those guys who didn't even mind solitary. Nothing scared him."

Another man, across the aisle, had overheard.

"Yeah," he added. "That was one crazy dude. I felt sorry for Sam, the guy who had to share with him. You could see Sam's number was up, and it was only a question of time."

"As long as Dolan doesn't come back here again, I'll stay," one of the others added, and there was raucous laughter from round about that echoed down the corridor.

Katie nodded. She wondered if Dolan had shared his plans for escape with Sam, and that was why he'd killed him. Sam might have known where he was headed or what he planned to do. It was the sign of an ice-cold psychopath to silence his confidant before fleeing. What a pity, this had been a dead-end, she thought.

Suddenly, the idea occurred to her. It was so sudden, so tempting, that she couldn't resist it.

She was actually down here, in the cells, where her sister's suspected killer was incarcerated. Perhaps she could take a minute to do what she'd always wanted to and confront him about the crime.

Katie took a deep breath, knowing she would have to be quick, because she didn't want to steal time away from this urgent investigation.

"What about Everton?" she asked.

The guard glanced at her in surprise, as if wondering how she knew that name.

"What about him?" the prisoner asked.

"I heard he knows things. He's a similar type of guy. Would he know?"

Looking shifty, the prisoner shrugged. "I can't say. Everton keeps to himself."

The guard spoke to her in a low voice. "Everton was in solitary for a month when he arrived. Since then, he's been in the maximum-security cells but he is in a cell on his own."

"What is he like?" Katie asked. It felt strange, straying to a place she knew she shouldn't go. But how could she not take the chance to know more about the man she believed was her sister's killer?

The guard shrugged. "Dolan was trouble, but Everton is weird. He hardly ever speaks to anyone. The warden has to order him to shower. He sits in his cell, day in, day out, staring at everyone, looking right through you. He stares at his reflection in the glass. It feels like he is waiting for someone to come through the other side."

Katie shivered. It was making her feel nauseous, hearing about the behavior of the monster who must have taken her sister. But now she felt driven to get face-to-face with him.

"Where is he?" she asked.

"He's all the way at the end of the row. Cell forty-two. He had no interaction with Dolan as they were managed separately."

"He knows me," Katie told the guard quietly. "I was involved in a trial with him, years ago. He might speak to me and give me some facts. Can you give us some privacy? Just for a minute?"

"I'll wait here," the guard agreed, stepping back.

This was her chance. The only one she might have, to speak to the man she was sure had killed her twin.

Adrenaline sizzled inside her as she headed to his cell.

Everton stood near the door, as if he was expecting her, and she wondered if he'd remembered her voice. The minute he saw her, she picked up recognition in his gaze.

He leaned against the wall, watching her. His appearance was intimidating. His eyes were cold and dark, his expression hard. His face was more lined than it had been in court. His hair was now threaded with gray. Otherwise, he was as tall and strong as she remembered.

Katie forced herself not to seem intimidated, reminding herself that she had been preparing for this moment for more than a decade.

"You know who I am?" she asked softly.

He nodded. "I remember you. From the trial." He smiled slightly.

She recalled that expression. It chilled her to the bone.

"You knew my twin? Josie?"

He paused for a long moment.

Then, to Katie's astonishment, he nodded silently.

He knew her! It was an admission he'd never made before. He'd denied it at trial.

Her heart sped up. Was she finally going to get the truth?

"What happened to her? What did you do to her?" she said in a low voice. She could hear it was shaking and knew he could, too, but there was no way she could sound calm. Not when asking this.

He looked at her for a long moment. It was difficult to read his expression. She was sure he was weighing up his options.

"You think I know what happened to her?" he said eventually.

"I think you do. And I think you killed her," she whispered. Her mouth felt dry.

He shrugged. "Maybe I did. Maybe I didn't. Is that why you're here? Because you think I killed your little sister?"

She glanced back at the guard. He was watching them, but at a distance. She felt as if she was walking a tightrope. That the wrong move would end in disaster, but that if she kept her balance, she might just reach the end.

"Yes," she said. "I believe you killed her, but I'd like to hear your version. You've been here a long time. I'm sure you remember. Perhaps now is a good time to share your memories with someone?"

"You don't know what happened to her yet, do you?" Everton said in a low whisper. "But I will tell you. She's the one who begged me to save her. She's the one I never killed," he sneered.

Katie felt the blood drain from her face. She couldn't believe what he was saying.

"You killed her. What's going on?"

But Everton moved away from the cell door, chuckling to himself in a low, unpleasant voice.

He walked over to the stainless-steel mirror and sat down in front of it.

Katie's mind was whirling. She couldn't make sense of what she'd been told. What did he mean by those words? Were any of them truthful?

Everton looked up at his reflection and his eyes met hers. He was staring through the glass. Staring straight at her. His expression was fierce, yet his eyes were alight with a strange, hypnotic flame.

"I see you," he said, and his words were so low she could barely hear him. He smiled, and it was a smile of triumph.

Katie felt took a step back, away from Everton, and met the gaze of the guard.

She guessed that this behavior meant he was done talking. And she didn't think she could handle anything more, anyway. Not now. Not after this bombshell.

Had he left her sister alive? Was she the one who never got killed?

Or was he just taunting her?

"You all right?" the guard asked. "You look shaken up."

Katie nodded. "I'll be all right," she said in a low voice.

But she wasn't. She felt sick. She was shaken by the conversation she'd had with Everton. She had no idea what to make of it.

At that moment, she heard hurried footsteps. Guiltily, she spun around, to see Leblanc rushing down the corridor toward them. He looked stressed.

"Did you get any information?" he asked. Katie could hear he was suspicious of why she was down here.

"Dolan only spoke to Sam, his cellmate, the man he later murdered." Katie replied. "The others were all afraid of him. He was violent and threatening."

"And that inmate?" He pointed to the cell. "I saw you speaking to him. Who was he?"

"Another serial killer. His name is Charles Everton," Katie said. She couldn't risk telling Leblanc anything more.

"Why were you speaking to him? He's at the other end of the prison and that would surely mean separate routines? You came here to interview Dolan's neighbors." Leblanc challenged.

Katie shrugged.

"Let's get out of here," Leblanc said tersely, leading the way outside.

She knew what he was thinking. He had seen her outside Everton's cell, but she was not going to tell him about the conversation. She could sense Leblanc was deeply suspicious.

She walked with him in silence, going over that exchange in her head again and again. She knew she would never stop thinking about what Everton had said. Had she been wrong about him from the beginning?

"Let's try and solve this case now, shall we? The guards at the gate saw nothing. The snow was blowing hard and there was a white-out. You have no information. I have no information. So far, this trip has been a waste of time and we'll have to answer to Scott," Leblanc sounded angry. His voice was low, but she could see that he was on the edge of losing control.

Katie knew she was firmly on the back foot. She'd messed up by sidetracking to Everton. Now her case partner didn't trust her, and they were no closer to locating a dangerous killer.

She had a lot of lost ground to make up and needed to do it fast.

CHAPTER SIX

Carl Dolan pushed the hood low over his face, whistling softly to himself through numb lips.

Two years since he'd tasted freedom. Two years too long. One careless moment was all it had taken. He knew, now. He'd learned from his mistakes. He didn't intend to go back inside. Ever.

He looked down at the piece of paper in his hand, checking the coordinates again. He'd memorized them as soon as he'd gotten them, but he always liked to be sure.

This small town was as dead as could be. He walked past a long row of shops that were still closed at this early hour. Large, silver padlocks had been locked over the doors. When the chill wind picked up, the padlocks rattled loudly in their steel loops. He looked at them and smiled. His memories were locked up too. Locked away in his mind, where they couldn't hurt him. He'd learned to live with them.

He walked up to the storefront of a place selling winter gear. The prison guard's uniform was warm, but it wasn't outdoor gear, and he was shivering. He needed to change. This store had what he was looking for.

He had to break in, but he'd do it by going around the back. Out of sight.

Dolan went around to the rear of the building, finding the emergency exit. People in this part of the world didn't take care. Nobody thought a robber would break in. They were far too trusting, up here in small towns in the cold north.

He felt a rush of hatred toward the small-town lifestyle, and the people who lived in these quaint little homes. They were nice people, who lived calm, secluded lives. They failed to see what was in front of them or else refused to see. They turned their backs on evil. They had turned their backs on him.

Carl Dolan was not a nice man. He knew he was a man who deserved to be locked away, locked up for life, but he was strong and smart enough to have broken out.

And on that bright, cold, winter morning, he knew he had to get his revenge.

He carefully felt for the latch and the door popped open, just as he knew it would. He pushed it open, slipped inside and closed it behind him. He stood still, listening and waiting.

Then he walked over to the sales counter. The cash register was closed. He grabbed a pen and forced it open, using the brute strength he'd taken care to build while in prison.

Two hundred dollars inside. He pocketed the cash and then turned to the clothing racks. He needed to steal something warm. Something unobtrusive, that would blend in.

As he did, a voice spoke out of nowhere.

"You're not good enough," it said. "You never will be. You're weak and ugly. You're a loser and I'm going to prove it."

He spun around, the hair on the back of his neck standing straight up.

"Who said that?" he asked, his voice high and tight.

The store was empty and silent.

"Who said that?" he repeated.

Nothing. Just a vague sense of menace in the air.

Dolan chose a thick beige coat, a scarf, gloves, warm pants, and heavy boots. All in neutral colors. He didn't want to stand out.

He stuffed the money into his pants pocket and left the store the same way he'd gotten in.

Back outside, his footsteps crunched on the snow-covered sidewalk. The freezing wind whipped at his coat, but he didn't notice. The new gear kept it at bay.

He glanced around him, making sure he was still unobserved. The street he was on was quiet and the few pedestrians in sight had their coats pulled up against the biting wind.

He had his plans set out. Now, he needed to put them into practice.

Ahead, at the crossroad, he saw a sign.

Niagara Falls 100 miles

That was where he needed to go. He knew he would find what he needed for the next step. But to get there, he could use a vehicle.

Ahead, across the intersection, he saw a truck stop with a gas station and a general store.

Dolan headed there purposefully, knowing what he was looking for. He needed to find a vehicle with Canadian plates. And he needed a driver that looked enough like him for people not to notice the difference at a glance. That shouldn't be too difficult because Dolan was average looking.

Dolan glanced around him. He was the only person on the street, but he sensed he was being watched. He knew that sensation. It was the one thing he'd never forgotten.

Paranoia rose up and he fought it back. He couldn't give in to it. That was the mistake he'd made last time. He'd hesitated and the cops had gotten to him. Now, he had a clear purpose.

He walked into the diner and sat down at the table nearest the window.

"What can I get you?" the tired-sounding waitress asked, shuffling over.

"Coffee," Dolan said, without looking at her. He was surveying the cars coming and going at the gas station.

A black Jeep with Canadian plates pulled into the lot.

Dolan sat straighter. He watched the driver climb out of the Jeep.

It was a woman. She was dressed in jeans and a baggy sweater. She started to fill her tank. He looked away as she glanced in his direction. He didn't need a woman.

There was an old truck with Canadian plates. Dolan stared eagerly. Would the driver look like him?

But the guy who swung out of the truck had a round face and a mustache. His nose was red from the cold. The Canadian started filling up with gas and Dolan resumed the search for new, better prospects.

Then another car pulled in. It was a sturdy, white Toyota SUV. The plates were right. He watched carefully. Would the driver be right?

The man climbed out and Dolan's eyes narrowed. He was slim, average height, and he looked enough like him.

The driver wasn't filling up with gas. Not yet. Instead, the guy was heading for the general store.

"Cancel the coffee," he said, standing up as the waitress brought it. She stared at him like he was dirt. He didn't care. She was lucky. In other circumstances he might have cared and then he would have made her sorry.

He headed across the street. But then he hesitated as he saw a shadow behind a car parked a few meters away.

"You shouldn't have come back," the voice said. "You're not welcome. You never were. You were always an outsider. You deserved everything you got.

It whispered directly in his ear.

Dolan spun around, searching for the speaker. He was sure the speaker was right there, right behind him.

But there was no one there.

Dolan walked quickly toward the store. His paranoia was forgotten. Now, as he put his plan into action, his mind was racing. He felt the sense of adrenaline he'd last experienced that morning in his cell, as he waited for the guards to arrive.

He had a utility knife he'd taken from the guard. It was the one thing he knew he would need. Now it was in his belt and its presence reassured him as he stared through the store window.

The Canadian was in there, right now. He watched him for a few more moments, making sure he was the right one. He didn't want to make a mistake. But even from closer, he looked similar enough. He had pale blue eyes, too.

The man was loading up on provisions, as if he didn't know what was going to happen to him. Now he was at the counter. He was paying the woman who worked behind it.

If Dolan could play his cards right, in the next few minutes, he'd have his own set of wheels and a passport to Canada.

The driver might not be so lucky. Dolan smiled a cruel smile. He knew he wouldn't be, because he would be dead.

CHAPTER SEVEN

Ten minutes' drive from the prison, Katie saw a rest stop with a gas station and a coffee shop.

"Shall we pull in here?" she asked. She'd been looking out for the closest warm place they could sit to discuss. This was it.

"Sure," Leblanc said in a surly tone.

Up until then they had driven in silence. There had been an uncomfortable atmosphere in the car. She knew Leblanc didn't trust her. She knew that he knew she was hiding something. The dynamic between them felt complicated and tense.

Climbing out, she saw this rest stop was in the middle of nowhere. It was on the main road, but there was hardly any traffic going by. It was surrounded by snowy hills and pine trees. The air was cold and still and smelled of pine. It spooked her to think that Dolan must be somewhere out here, at large and dangerous.

A couple of cars were parked at gas pumps and a lone truck was stopped in the lot. But they were the only ones who had chosen to go inside.

The small coffee shop was at the side of the gas station. It was squashed between the gas pumps and the parking lot, as if it didn't have much room to breathe.

Walking in, Katie saw a table in the corner where she and Leblanc could talk in privacy should any other customers arrive. It felt good to be out of that car. She needed a dose of caffeine and some warmth in the atmosphere, and she wasn't even thinking of the frigid weather, but rather the tension between her and her partner.

"What would you like?" the waitress asked politely, hurrying over.

"Coffee, with cream and sugar, please," Katie said, feeling she needed an energy boost.

"The same," Leblanc added, looking straight at Katie. His gaze was cold and penetrating. She looked away.

The waitress disappeared back into the kitchen.

Then, Katie turned her attention back to Leblanc.

She could sense that he was trying to read her. She tried to stay cool. She had no reason to feel guilty. Whatever he was imagining, she was determined that she wasn't going to tell him. Her past was private. It was hers alone.

"This trip has been a waste of time," Leblanc said. "I spoke to the guards at the prison exit and they both thought he went south."

"The direction he took when he left means nothing," Katie insisted, guilt and frustration warring inside her.

"Surely he was just trying to get away, as far and fast as he could." Leblanc sounded frustrated. "The authorities, the US Marshals, also think south would be the logical choice. That's where they're focusing their search."

"What about the more important reason. His motives for breaking out of jail? Where's he going to want to go and who's he going to want to see? He might well have unfinished business."

"What motive would he have, other than getting free?" Leblanc asked. Now he sounded more curious than angry.

"He's a serial killer. Their minds don't work like ours. Most of them feel more comfortable within a certain geography and that's their killing ground. They may have multiple motives for committing murders. We don't know Dolan's motives yet, but we know he has killed in Canada, and the far north of the US. That's his territory and it's where he'll return," Katie insisted, wishing Leblanc would accept her argument.

He nodded grimly as if this did provide food for thought.

"I messaged Scott when we left the prison and asked him to send through more details on Dolan's criminal record," Leblanc said, as the coffee arrived. "It should come through any minute. He's sending it to both of us. When it arrives, we can confirm that."

At that moment, Katie's phone pinged.

She opened the mail and drew in a long breath while she read. Dolan had left a trail of death and destruction behind him before finally being caught.

Katie scanned the details. She couldn't get past the shock of how vicious he was. As she recalled from the meeting with Scott, he had begun killing at the age of twenty. Now, he was thirty years old, and had killed seven times, as far as the police knew. What she hadn't yet known was that most of his murders had taken place in public places, or out on the street. He was bold and quick and unafraid.

Katie thought about his mindset. Had he escaped just to get free from prison? Or was there a bigger motive for his breakout? Surely there was information in this report that could help her predict where he would go?

She scrolled through the report, taking in the details. And then something caught her eye.

"Look here, Leblanc," she said.

"What is it?"

"He had seven kills but was busy with the eighth. However, he didn't kill the last victim. Edith Jackson. He injured her and she got away. She hid in a shed, and while he was hunting for her, the police arrived. That's how Dolan eventually got caught."

Leblanc's eyes widened.

"That's significant."

"He could be targeting her next, looking to finish what he started."

"That's definitely worth following up." Leblanc sounded worried now. "Where does Edith Jackson live?"

"According to this report, her recorded address was in Jamestown, New York."

"South of the prison," Leblanc observed triumphantly.

"But she could have moved, especially after an incident like that. I'd be surprised if she didn't," Katie shot back.

"Let's find out," Leblanc said, as he picked up the phone and dialed Scott's number.

"Can you trace us an address?" he said. "Edith Jackson, who resided in Jamestown, New York, two years ago. She was Dolan's last attempted victim."

He waited, listened. Then he scribbled in the notebook before disconnecting.

"She moved," he said. "She now lives in Fairport, just outside Rochester. That's about two hours away from here."

"To the north," Katie noted, feeling she had to say it. Leblanc glowered.

"We need to cover both bases," Katie decided. "Let's ask Scott to send local police to Edith's previous address in Jamestown, in case he goes there. But we need to assume he knows where she moved, and get to her new address as fast as we can. If Dolan managed to get a ride, he could already be there."

*

With the lights and siren on, Katie pulled up outside number 3 Village Road, Fairport, an hour and fifty minutes later.

Adrenaline rushed through her as she jumped out of the car. There were already two police vehicles outside Edith's home from the Fairport Police Department. A young, anxious-looking cop climbed out of the car as soon as he saw them.

"Morning. We have a problem," he said immediately.

"What's happened?" Katie feared the worst. Had he already gotten to her? Were they too late?

"We don't know where Edith Jackson is. She's not at home. Not answering her phone."

Katie felt her stress multiply. She stared at the small house, so quiet and tranquil looking, under a grim and cloudy sky. Wind rustled the leaves of the juniper bush near the home's red mail box.

As the thought of Edith's danger sank in, Katie forgot her own problems.

"Any sign of a break-in?" she asked, wanting to get the clearest possible picture.

"There's no sign of forced entry. We can't confirm that she's been abducted."

"Does she work?"

"Yes, she works at Mario's, a restaurant in town, but she did the early shift today. By the time we got there, she'd gone."

"Her car?"

"It's an old Honda. We've got an alert out for the plates."

Katie was starting to feel sick. Where was Edith? She glanced at Leblanc, but he wasn't looking at her. Turning away, he strode toward the house with the other local cop. As she watched, the two men headed around it, peering through the windows.

Katie stayed by the road, scanning the neighborhood, looking for any sign of movement.

At that moment, she saw an elderly white Honda turn the corner.

She drew in a huge breath. Was this Edith? She rushed over to the car to confirm this was the woman they wanted.

"Edith Jackson?"

The driver was pretty and blond, in her mid-twenties, and she had a scared expression on her face. Katie saw a long scar on her neck.

"That's me." She wound down the window.

"It's Katie Winter, FBI. We've been looking for you."

"I was shopping. What's going on?" she asked. Katie could see Edith's adrenaline was surging as much as her own.

"Can you get out of the car? We need to talk to you."

"What's happening?" Edith sounded terrified now. Staring around her, she reached the inevitable conclusion.

"It's him, isn't it? Dolan? Has he escaped? Is that why you're here?" Her hand moved automatically to the scar on her neck. Katie felt a surge of sympathy for this woman, being forced to relive her trauma and terror again.

"Let's go inside and talk," Katie said, as calmly as she could.

Edith scrambled out of the car. She was shaking all over.

"He's going to get me."

"Nobody is going to get you now." Grasping her arm, Katie led her to the gate.

"Dolan. He's going to kill me," Edith insisted. She was sobbing as she walked.

Katie helped Edith into the house. She and Leblanc headed into a small living room while one cop kept watch at the door. Nobody was taking any chances with a man this dangerous.

The walls of the room were decorated with cheap but colorful art and tapestries. Although the furnishings were shabby and second-hand, there were flowers in a vase on the mantle, and a few photographs on the coffee table.

Katie thought the house was warm and welcoming. It was a great improvement on her bare apartment. Perhaps she should decorate, she wondered. If Edith could rebuild peace and beauty into her life after the ordeal she'd been through, surely she could, too?

"Did anything feel wrong today? Did you receive any missed calls, any unusual messages? Did you suspect you were being watched or followed at all?" Katie asked.

"I don't think I was followed. Everything seemed normal until I saw the cops here. I left work and went shopping, and forgot my phone charger," Edith explained. "But everything seemed normal on that - that day, too." She shivered.

"I understand," Katie said.

"I don't want to have to hide from him again. I've been living in fear of this happening. I have nightmares, almost every night." She bit her lip hard.

"There's no evidence he's been here," Leblanc reassured her. "But the local police will put you in a safe house and keep you there under police protection until he's caught."

Tears sparkled in Edith's eyes. She nodded in agreement.

Even though this was a dead end, Katie had one more question that she hoped might provide insight.

"Did you know Dolan before he attempted to murder you?" she asked.

Edith nodded. "Yes. We worked at the same gas station. Not for long, though. Soon after I was hired, he was fired, for absenteeism and lateness. He also killed the gas station owner who fired him. He was the last victim, I believe. I think he thought I'd stolen his job. That's what he said to me anyway."

Katie nodded.

Thanks to this, she could now start to see Dolan's pattern of killing.

He had targeted people that he believed, in his mind, had done him wrong. He had been looking for revenge.

So that was a direction they urgently needed to pursue.

CHAPTER EIGHT

Dave Bradshaw walked out of the general store, carrying his bag of supplies. Chocolate, Cheetos, and Coke. The three essential Cs for any road trip, no matter the time of year. It was a long drive up to Ontario and he'd started later than he'd meant to.

At any rate, his family time was done, and he could be glad of that. Family was a stress. He was glad he lived in Ontario, and not in New York, where they resided.

He hated his ex-wife and wanted nothing to do with her. But he had to talk to her once a year, when the alimony was discussed. It was a waste of time and had been for the last twelve years. She never listened to him; she just talked at him.

Dave opened the door and put the bag of snacks on the floor behind the seat. Then he got into the truck and started the engine.

At that moment, he heard a knock on his window.

He looked out.

A brown-haired, unassuming man in a taupe coat was standing there, twiddling his fingers uneasily.

Dave buzzed the window down impatiently, wondering what he wanted. He didn't have time for random strangers today.

"This is embarrassing to ask," the man said. "But I need a ride. My car broke down, and there's no sign of the tow truck, and my daughter's getting home from school in half an hour. She won't be able to get inside if I'm not there."

Dave hesitated. He didn't want to get involved in other people's business. He wasn't even the kind of guy who sprang for sob stories. His first instinct was to say no, but the guy seemed so anxious.

"Where are you going?" he asked with a sigh.

"It's just a few miles down the road."

"All right. I'll take you that far. Get in," he said grudgingly.

"Thanks. That's very kind. I can pay you for the gas." The man scrambled inside.

"No need," Dave shook his head. Did this idiot think he couldn't afford his own gas, he wondered irritably.

"Thank you, thank you so much, you have no idea how much I appreciate it." The man gave Dave a sheepish grin.

In sullen silence, Dave pulled off, and turned the SUV onto the motorway.

As he drove, he thought again of his ex-wife and her unreasonable demands. She had accused him of hitting her. That was untrue. He'd never raised a hand to her. Well, only the once.

He'd had enough of her lies. He was tired of this court system and tired of her ongoing need for money. He would take her down. She wanted people to think he was a wife beater. He'd have to put a stop to that.

This divorce was supposed to be permanent; it was supposed to be final. And yet, he had to go through this rigmarole every year. It was humiliating.

Dave had had enough. He wasn't paying her any more money.

He was going to make her see reason. This was the last time he was going through this crap. She'd better understand that. And he'd had enough of his toxic family, too. His cousin had wanted a ride to the border. Dave had refused. That was the only reason he'd had an empty seat now, in his two-seater cab. Perhaps it had been the reason he'd felt guilty enough to offer this asshole a ride, a decision he was now regretting.

"How much further?" he asked the man in the passenger seat, suddenly tired of doing a stranger a favor.

The man didn't answer. Instead, he began to tap his fingers rhythmically on his knees.

Dave was annoyed. Who did this guy think he was? He'd given him a ride. The least he could do was keep still and not act restless. It wasn't like Dave was driving slowly.

"Not far, really," the man said. "Thank you, thank you very much."

The man continued to tap his fingers on his knees. He didn't even look in Dave's direction.

Dave was getting irritated by this point. He wanted the guy to stop fidgeting.

"What's not far? I've gone far enough," he said. He had a sudden desire to dump this man in the snow. He wasn't one for good deeds.

The guy burst out laughing. Not a chuckle. A hearty laugh. It didn't sound as if he were laughing at anything in particular, but that he was laughing for laughter's sake.

Dave felt suddenly uncomfortable, and shivered, turning up the heater because the car felt suddenly chilled. He was deeply regretting his decision to give this guy a ride.

He decided to wait until he'd gotten over whatever he found so funny, and then he was going to tell this idiotic creep he wasn't taking him any further, and that he could get out and wait for another ride in the snow.

With a snort, the guy finally controlled himself. After his outburst of laughter, he sat very still. It almost felt to Dave as if he was listening to something that Dave couldn't hear.

Dave turned on the radio, loudly. He'd give him something to listen to. His nerves were frayed, and he was ready to pull over and tell the guy to get out. Then he could go and catch a bus, or whatever.

"Listen, dude, my patience has run out," he snapped. "Where's this place you said was near here?"

"You'll see it in a few minutes," the man said. "I'll tell you where to go. Just a few miles further. Not long, not long." He rubbed his hands together and then thrust them out in front of him, as if they were on fire.

"What's the name of this town?" he challenged him. If he couldn't give him a name, he was throwing him out, right now. He had never wanted to give a ride to this idiot. Was he filming him, he wondered suddenly? Was he going to be part of some joke YouTube video? "Tell me the name, or I'm stopping now."

"Okay," the man said quickly. "You can stop right here."

Dave checked his mirrors automatically. Nothing behind him or in sight. But nothing around him, either.

He braked to a halt, feeling suspicious.

"Get out," he snapped.

And in the next moment, everything went haywire. The guy didn't climb out as Dave had expected him to. He turned and stared at him, with a blank expression in his pale eyes.

Then he lunged at Dave and grabbed on to him.

"Whoa! What the hell are you doing?" Dave exclaimed.

It took a moment for Dave to realize that the man was holding a knife at his throat.

"What the hell?" His voice sounded high and scared. Not like him at all. And the guy in the passenger seat suddenly seemed very strong. Very focused. Not the weird, laughing, overly apologetic person Dave had thought he was.

"Out," the man said, and his words were as icy as the air.

He opened the door and pushed Dave out. The man was strong and wiry. He had his arm wrapped tight around Dave's throat.

Dave struggled, flailing as the guy dragged him toward the ditch. He couldn't believe this. He was so strong, and he had him by the throat. How had he done that? Why had he not fought him off in time?

Now he was being choked. He was going to be murdered. There was nothing he could do.

Dave thrashed violently, trying to get a hold on the guy, to pull him away so he stopped choking him. It was the middle of nowhere. No passing cars. Nobody to see or help him.

He struggled vainly, but he couldn't breathe. The snow felt icy against his skin. His own decisions had brought him here and now it was too late.

He was going to die here. He was going to die by some lunatic's hand.

The man was not laughing now. He was staring at him with a blank expression as he squeezed.

"I'm sorry," he said. "Sorry, dude. I didn't want to do this, but I needed you. I needed to become you."

Dave stared at him, his eyes wide and confused. He barely heard the words.

A few more snowflakes landed on Dave's face, as gently as feathers. Then the next ones hit harder. They stung his skin.

But the next ones, he didn't feel at all.

CHAPTER NINE

Katie had hoped things would be different as they headed back to the car. She felt they had a new direction to look in. If he'd started targeting people for revenge, they needed to research other potential victims, and fast.

But it seemed Leblanc was ready for an argument, and not convinced by Katie's logic.

"I think going north is pointless," he insisted. "He didn't come for Edith, did he? I've just checked my phone and Scott has reported there's no sign of him at her old place, either. So he isn't trying to get her. He's been in prison two years and could have changed his modus operandi by now."

She glanced at him from the corner of her eye. He was in the passenger seat, staring straight ahead. She didn't know how to react. He was being so stubborn. Everything about him screamed 'stubborn.'

"Listen, the theory of revenge is the only idea we have," Katie argued.

"We don't have anything stronger than a feeling. We have no evidence that he's still pursuing it. Every cop in the state is on this thing, and we have nothing. If you're looking into his background, where are you going to start?" he snapped. "The guy was a job hopper. He was probably fired from, or quit, ten different jobs in his life, and those are just the ones listed in the document. There might be many more. He was arrested numerous times on lesser charges. He could also have an issue with those police."

"So what do you mean by that?" she argued.

"I mean the parameters are far too wide. We can't start looking back at his entire life. We'll be running around the country for months!"

"We still need to start somewhere," Katie said. "We have to look at his mindset."

They were sitting in the car. She hadn't even started it up yet.

"I also read through the records. Some of his victims are totally random. He killed some people he had issues with. But he also killed people who were just in his way. I think that's where we need to focus.

On his escape route. Where he would have gone when he left prison and where he plans to hide," Leblanc insisted.

"I think you're wrong," she answered calmly. She didn't want to get into an argument with him now. She had decided that an argument would be pointless.

"I think you're wrong. And I don't trust your reasoning, Katie."

"Why's that?" she flashed back, hurt and defensive.

"Because you've been on your own agenda from the time we started this case. What were you doing in the prison, talking to that random lifer?" Now he sounded seriously angry.

"Why are you questioning my reasons? Do you not trust me?"

"No. I don't trust you, after that stunt."

Her heart sank. It felt like he had punched her in the gut. She wanted to say something to justify her actions but couldn't get the words out of her mouth.

"I have big questions. And it's clear you can't answer them," he snapped.

Perhaps they weren't going to be able to cooperate on this case, Katie realized, feeling a sense of doom as she stared at Leblanc's strong, set jaw. Her partner didn't trust her. And she didn't trust him enough to tell him what she knew she should. It felt too late, now. He was angry. If she tried now, he wouldn't listen.

Katie felt sick to her stomach. It was awkward between them, and she couldn't talk to him the way she had done on their previous case.

"Look," she said.

She didn't know how to verbalize what she wanted to say. That it wasn't working between them. They needed different case partners. That the cooperation that had driven them forward on their last case had vanished, replaced with mistrust.

"I think we're not a great fit," she said, feeling the words hurt more than she had expected.

"What do you mean?" he asked incredulously.

"I mean I don't think we're a good team," she said, still staring out at the snow. "We're not working together like we need to. Either we need to change that, or we need to get a different dynamic going."

He nodded sourly. He didn't show any desire to change things.

"Maybe we should go back now. Tell Scott we're off this case. Look at the crimes in our local jurisdiction. We only came here because you had ulterior motives. I suggest we drive straight to the airport and get on a plane."

Stubborn to the last breath, Katie thought in utter frustration. And maybe that was her fault, too, she worried inwardly.

When her phone rang, loud in the silence, they both jumped. She groped for it in her purse.

It was Scott.

"We may have a new development," he said, his voice sharp. Immediately, Katie switched this to speaker, glancing at Leblanc. She saw his anger disappear as he heard Scott's words.

"What's happened?" she asked.

"A body's been found on the 219 highway heading north, near one of the rest stops. I'll send you the coordinates. It's an unidentified man. No car, no wallet, but he was strangled. I'm going to send you visuals now, and a description, so you can see what he looked like."

Katie glanced at Leblanc. This was a significant twist. She was sure this must be Dolan's work. He was heading somewhere. He'd wanted a car, a wallet, and an ID. Now he had everything he needed. The chase was on.

"We'll get there as soon as we can," she said.

"I told you, he was wanting to hide. Not take revenge," Leblanc said triumphantly as soon as she'd disconnected the call.

Feeling annoyed, Katie shot back, "You predicted he'd go south. This is north. And he's killing to get where he wants to go, because that's who he is. Ice cold. It doesn't mean revenge is not on his mind."

"You're wrong," Leblanc insisted.

A moment later, her phone beeped with the coordinates.

She checked them on her map and set off immediately, trying not to feel annoyed by her partner's combative attitude.

The murder site was a half-hour's drive from the prison, she calculated. How had he planned the kill in that area?

"If he took the victim's ID, he must have stolen it from someone similar looking. So he couldn't just have been hitching on the road," she theorized. "It's more likely he would have staked someone out at a rest stop. Waited for the right person, begged a ride, and then jumped them."

Leblanc nodded. "I've just got the visuals of the victim from the scene," he said. "You're right. This man is similar looking. His eyes are pale blue, and he has the same shade of brown hair, longer than Dolan's but otherwise similar. Their face shape is similar. And they look to be more or less the same age. He wanted to become this guy, whoever he is. Now, we have to find out his name, and urgently."

"Especially if Dolan's looking to get over the border," Katie agreed.

Leblanc was now using his cop logic to plan their actions.

"I think we should stop by the scene first. See if there's any further evidence. They might have something useful by the time we get there."

"Agreed," Katie said.

"Then, from there, our quickest solution is going to be to pull the camera footage from the nearest rest stops. I agree he must have used that as his hunting ground. Let's start there and see what the footage tells us. Hopefully we can see the guy's face on it, if he stopped for gas, or went in to buy supplies."

Katie felt a strange, curious calm as she reached the highway, turning her lights and siren on. At least they knew they were now going in the right direction.

She was no longer feeling the crushing sense of guilt she had felt only a couple of hours earlier. She had made mistakes; she had veered off track and she had rightfully made her partner distrustful. But they would work through it. They would solve this.

Of course, that all depended on whether they could get a visual ID on the murdered man in time. He'd gotten a lead on them and would be gaining fast. She felt anxious as she calculated how long it would take to get there.

If they traveled in heavy traffic, they would be up against the clock, even with the siren. The icy roads were dangerous. Fast driving would be risky, but every second counted now, Katie knew, as she accelerated smoothly onto the icy road.

Dolan had killed already, to obtain a new ID. But he'd left the body out in the open. If he'd hidden it away, it would have taken them far longer to start the hunt.

Why had he done that, Katie wondered.

Had it just been a mistake, or was there another reason?

After what he'd done so far since he'd left the solitary cell, she knew that underestimating Carl Dolan would be a serious, and perhaps fatal, mistake.

CHAPTER TEN

Leblanc felt a sense of doom as he saw the red and blue flashing lights appear out of the gray-white gloom ahead. They had reached the scene. Dolan had fled north, and he'd killed again as soon as he needed to.

Now, they had to work fast. He felt the pressure of a ticking clock and knew they had to get some answers.

The windshield of their unmarked was fogging up in the intense cold. Leblanc wiped it yet again with his sleeve, while Katie bumped her way over the packed snow in the emergency lane, easing the car up to the barrier.

"Let's see what we have," he said. The more clues they could find at this scene, the better their chances of catching up with him.

He climbed out, shivering as he walked over to the knot of officers wearing yellow safety vests. Flapping in the breeze, the crime scene tape looked oddly bright against the dark and ominous sky.

"Winter and Leblanc from the special task force," Katie introduced herself. The lead detective nodded a grim greeting.

"How did you find the body?" was Leblanc's first question.

"A passing motorist saw it. Stopped, took a look, and called us immediately."

Stepping aside, the detective gave them their first view of what Leblanc was sure was Dolan's latest victim.

There had been little attempt to hide the body. It was no wonder it had been seen. This crime had been quick and dirty, with speed the main objective, he guessed. In his dark trench coat, the deceased man was easily visible, sprawled face-up on the snowy bank to the right of the highway.

"He was strangled," said the hard-faced detective.

"Any idea how recent?" Leblanc asked, wondering how much time they still had, or else had lost.

" My feeling is that this is very recent," the detective said. "This road carries light traffic at this time of day, and I don't think too many people would have driven straight past an obvious dead body by the side of the road."

Leblanc nodded. His logic made sense. Even if a driver hadn't wanted to stop, they would still have called 911.

"Do we know who he is?" Katie asked.

The detective shook his head.

"No ID. Nothing personal on him at all."

The air filled with a new noise: a helicopter. It appeared over the top of the ridge on the other side of the highway. It hovered low over the scene. Then it moved slowly along the highway.

Leblanc saw three technicians were unloading equipment from the van. He knew they would be processing the scene and taking any evidence to the lab.

"What about the car tire tracks? Do they tell us anything?" he asked.

"Take a look," the detective said.

They scrunched a few paces over the snow.

"These tracks are from the motorist that stopped," the officer pointed out. "And these ones are from the vehicle that the victim must have been inside. The snow is disturbed where the victim was pulled out and killed. Then he was dragged a couple of yards and left there. So we have footprints and tire tracks."

"The two sets of tracks look similar width," Leblanc said, gazing down at the marks which were clear in the snow.

"The tracks are a similar width and depth, which points to the fact the carjacked vehicle was also an SUV. Not that this narrows it down," the detective said, lifting his woolen hat to rub his head. "Most cars on the road this time of year, going up north, are this type."

"Are there cameras anywhere along the route?" Katie asked.

"The last camera is on a bridge about twenty miles back. It seems to be operational, but the footage might be obscured if it was snowing hard. Even so, I've requested footage for the past two hours."

"We need to get ahead of this," Leblanc said aloud, glancing at Katie. "How far away is the closest rest stop that this driver would have passed?"

"Twenty minutes' drive back from here," the detective said.

Now that they knew they were looking for an SUV, the parameters had narrowed, and every detail helped them.

"Let's go there now and check it," he said.

*

When they arrived at the small rest stop, Leblanc saw it was basic, and had only a few facilities. The victim could have used the restroom, gone into the coffee shop, or else bought provisions from the general store on the other side of the forecourt.

"I'll check this side; you check the other?" Katie suggested, and Leblanc nodded agreement. He headed straight over to the general store, opened the door, and walked inside, together with a blast of wind that rustled the Cheetos packets on the stand by the door.

"Police," he said, showing his badge. "We are following up on a carjacking and murder that occurred north of here. We need to see your footage."

"Sure." The owner looked surprised and apprehensive. "A murder? You think the killer came in here?"

"I'm hoping to see the victim," Leblanc explained. "We need an ID on him."

"Okay." Nodding in understanding, the man walked out from behind the counter. "Let's get onto that straight away. I'll download it onto the computer in the corner."

Leblanc followed the man to an elderly PC on the counter at the back of the store. Working quickly, in a few moments, he'd pulled up the footage.

"How far back must I go?" he asked.

Leblanc remembered the local cops had said they didn't think the body could have been there long.

"Let's start from an hour and a half ago and work forward," Leblanc decided.

The owner agreed and Leblanc watched the time scroll down the screen. They watched in silence, waiting to see if they could see the man they were looking for. He was grateful that the footage was in color, but it was grainy. Remembering the man's black trench coat, Leblanc made a note to look out for it.

"Can you freeze that?" Leblanc asked, spotting a similar looking garment.

He stared at the image carefully. It was a man in a dark coat. Leblanc could see his brown hair. The time checked out. This looked to be their guy.

"This customer. How did he pay?"

"Let me look at the time." After checking it, the owner hurried back to the till.

Let him have paid by card, Leblanc prayed. They urgently needed a break on this case. Every minute that passed made it more likely the killer would already have crossed the border.

While he waited, Leblanc ran through more of the footage. He didn't see any other customer who matched Dolan's physical description, within the next half-hour.

At that moment, the store owner called out.

"Sir, he paid by card. Here's the imprint. It's in the name of Dave A. Bradshaw. It's a Scotiabank card."

So the victim had been a Canadian citizen, heading home. Finally, they had a solid lead.

Leblanc felt energized as he rushed out of the rest stop and powered across the forecourt to where Katie was already hurrying to meet him.

"We've got an ID," he said. "We can pull up his vehicle's details on the way. The guy's a Canadian citizen so he was heading for the border. So that's where Dolan is going. If he stole a car on this highway, he's most likely heading up to Niagara Falls."

This crime was now firmly in their jurisdiction

"How fast can we get to the border?" Katie asked, sounding as excited and purposeful as Leblanc now felt.

"It's going to be too long a drive. Let's get a ride in the police helicopter," he said.

CHAPTER ELEVEN

The chopper blades cut through the snowy air as the helicopter lifted off, banking sharply before heading north. Katie stared through the window as the road scrolled beneath them, the blacktop a thin, dark squiggle against the white.

They were catching up, but would they be in time?

The sun had already set. It was six-thirty p.m. Dolan had been at large for almost twelve hours.

Over the noise of the chopper blades, Leblanc made a shouted phone call to Scott, briefing him on the latest updates.

"We have an ID on the vehicle already. It's a white Toyota SUV. I'll send you through the plates. Guy's name is Dave A. Bradshaw. Notify border control. If he's seen, if he tries to cross, he must be arrested instantly. No questions asked."

Katie wondered what Dolan was thinking. Even in the urgency of this chase, she needed to get inside his head. He was heading for the border, going back to his old killing ground. He was using a stolen ID, but now they knew whose it was.

Had he thought he would be able to cross before they caught up? What was his logic?

The drive through the plunging canyon of the Niagara River Gorge was breathtaking. She stared out the window as the river churned a mile below.

"What are we missing?" she asked. "We need to outthink this guy."

He must know he would be followed after dumping a victim by the roadside. Did he have another plan in place, she wondered?

"He could be panicking. Just aiming to get across as soon as he can," Leblanc shouted back, sounding hopeful.

"He dumped the body for a reason. It's a distraction. He's already thinking about what he's going to do next," Katie said.

"Well, you're the one who's kept up with his logic so far," Leblanc pointed out.

"This guy is ruthless but he's no fool. He's a planner. He thinks about the decision, he makes it, then he acts."

"And why here? Why not the wilderness?"

"When I looked at his file, I noticed that he's not scared to kill in public places. Some of his kills have been that way in the past. Maybe he even gets a thrill from it. He'll blend in easily among the tourists and foreigners at Niagara Falls. He might even kill again," she said somberly.

The lights from the border shone up ahead and she stared down at them. Katie was only too well aware that they could have a killer on the loose already. He could be armed. If he needed to cross the border, he might try anything to achieve his aims. And that would be the moment of truth for her and Leblanc. Could they stop him first?

As the chopper descended, Katie looked down on the traffic jam of cars, buses, and trucks. The roads and sidewalks were packed with tourists. They craned their necks, looking out at the frozen torrent of the Falls.

The helicopter landed, the sweeping blades gradually slowing. It had been a chilly ride and Katie prepared herself for an even icier temperature outside.

Now, they needed to find out if her predictions were correct. Would there be any sign of Dolan here at Niagara Falls, and would he try to cross the border?

The Canadian Border Services Agency had already been alerted by Scott. As soon as their feet hit the tarmac, Katie saw three border guards hurrying over to meet them. As she walked from the helipad toward them, she could see a line of traffic backed up on the road. The border guards managing the traffic had clearly been briefed. They were tense and businesslike as they stood by the scanner. One by one, they waved the cars through.

"We've put an alert out to all officers," the guard in charge told them. "We've been on high alert since we got your warning. We're on the lookout for a man fitting Dolan's description, as well as the vehicle you called in."

"He may be armed, and is definitely dangerous," Leblanc cautioned.

Katie couldn't get her mind off the thought that they could be too late. The killer could already be in Canada.

The guards led them to a small room at the back of the building. After the helicopter ride, the cold nipped at her face, making her cheeks numb.

The room was an operations room, small and cramped. Inside, another border guard was already on the computer and two more were watching the footage. Ranks of camera screens flashed up a constant procession of passing faces and vehicle plates.

"Is there any sign of him up to now?" Leblanc asked.

"Nothing on this side at all. No one fitting that description has been seen crossing the bridge. We also haven't seen a vehicle with those plates as yet."

"Are we sure he's not already across?" Leblanc asked.

"He hasn't crossed yet," the officer replied. "We pulled all the footage for the past hour. No vehicle of that description has passed, and passport control hasn't seen Dave A. Bradshaw go through. We've double checked all our systems."

The border guards had copies of the Toyota's plates and they were already checking them against the license databases.

Katie felt a flicker of hope. Could they have beaten Dolan here? Could they have caught him while he was still on the US side?

Perhaps he'd been too confident. And now, thanks to that, he would find himself trapped here.

Katie sat and watched the screen as the minutes ticked by. Leblanc paced about impatiently. The office was noisy with voices, the crackle of radios and the trill of phones as the border guards conferred with one another.

The video clips ran continually, but with every moment that passed, she had a feeling their chances were lessening. She felt uneasy. She knew Leblanc felt the same way. There was no way of knowing when the killer would cross the border, but logically, by now, he should have tried. Especially since he'd surely known they would catch up with him soon.

Where was he?

Katie took a deep breath and focused her thoughts. Now she needed to solve this puzzle, which she could do by thinking like him and trying to keep up with his intelligent, evil mind.

How would a killer like Dolan plan to cross the border, knowing he was already being scrutinized by police?

She found herself thinking of a magician, who would use sleight of hand to perform his tricks, making the audience focus on one point while he maneuvered elsewhere. She had a feeling that with the body left so obviously in the road, Dolan might be planning a similar strategy.

"I don't think he's going to cross," Katie said. "Not under this identity. He would have been here already. I think this whole move was preplanned. He wanted us to think he's coming here as Dave Bradshaw."

"What do you mean?" Leblanc asked.

"I think he's either going to cross at a different location, or as a different person. The second option means, while we're looking for Dave Bradshaw, he's holing up and hiding and planning to kill again. Grab a different victim. Get hold of a new identity."

"We can't risk that happening," Leblanc said emphatically.

"No," Katie said. "We have to start searching for him now. We can't allow him to hide. We need to organize a manhunt. Wherever he's hiding, we need to find him, before he does what I think he must be planning."

Leblanc nodded.

"Let's get that going straight away," he said, standing up and striding out of the office.

CHAPTER TWELVE

The personnel involved in the manhunt quickly assembled in the lobby of the border control office. Katie saw that there were ten guards taking part, as well as her and Leblanc. She worried it wouldn't be enough. Not for this man.

Leblanc turned to the border guards.

"Who's in charge here?" he asked.

"That would be me," a man said, stepping forward. He was in his forties, authoritative and with a military bearing.

"What's the name, Sergeant?" Leblanc asked.

"Sergeant Harkness," he replied, his tone brisk and businesslike.

"We need to systematically search the entire Niagara Falls area, Sergeant. We must search for any sign of him or his vehicle. It's imperative we find this man before he kills again."

The border guards nodded. Katie sensed a feeling of tension and urgency in the group. Nobody wanted to be responsible for another death.

"We're on it, sir," Harkness said, his tone firm and determined.

"He may well have changed vehicles," Katie cautioned. "He could be anywhere by now. He's resourceful and we need to keep that in mind. He crossed the border a few times before he went to prison, so he is definitely familiar with the area. He might be hiding his tracks or laying low. We need to set up a perimeter check. Please do not underestimate him."

A uniformed border guard nodded.

"We need to search all the places where he could hide, and we must form teams to check out all the local lodgings," she explained. "Do we have more manpower available?"

"Yes. We've pulled officers off other duties and they will be here soon. We should have double the numbers in another half-hour," Harkness said.

"Good," Leblanc said.

"Also, he may turn on that stolen cellphone at some stage, so we need to look out for its signal," Katie added.

Harkness turned to the border guards.

"Let's get to work."

Everyone jumped into action. The border guards clustered around the maps of the area, highlighting the locations where they would start their search.

"I think we need to split up now to cover more ground," Katie said quietly to Leblanc, hoping that after the events of the afternoon so far, he would be more trusting of her decisions. "I have a feeling he's looking for where people congregate. He's going to hide in the crowds and spot somebody else who looks similar to him, so he can switch identities a second time. And that's where he'll plan to kill again."

The best place to hide a needle was in a haystack. He'd choose a place where he could blend in and be inconspicuous.

He nodded. "I'll start to the west of here. There are quite a few parking areas and restaurants where pedestrians are moving."

"I'm going to go down to the Falls and the visitor's center," she said.

*

The wind was strong on the American side of the Falls. Across the border, the sky was cloudy and the Falls were a distant, imposing sight, the spray whipped up by the freezing wind and the spray frozen in a cloud surrounding the tall waterfalls.

Katie stood on the promenade, looking around, trying to immerse herself in the scene while keeping her eyes wide open for Dolan. Although it was getting late, the Falls was still busy. Restaurants were abuzz, and the cold didn't dampen the atmosphere at all. The vista that spread before her took her breath away, even though she had seen it before.

The winter air was icy and her skin was numb, but she didn't notice it as she surveyed the crowds.

She felt unnerved by his behavior and his uncanny ability to evade capture. Based on that, if he was here, he was going to kill again. She just had to find him first.

She headed down the promenade toward the visitor's center. Every time she passed a knot of tourists, she looked for Dolan in the faces of the onlookers.

And then she saw him.

A medium-height figure, swathed in a brown coat, walking on the far side of the promenade. The face shape clued her. It was identical to the killer's. And she had a glimpse of pale blue eyes before he pushed past.

She turned, her heart accelerating. This man wasn't behaving like a tourist. He was looking furtive, moving swiftly, checking behind him.

Ignoring the looks of people around her, she started after him. She had to get to him.

She ran after him, her feet flying over the icy sidewalk, her lungs working hard, her blood pumping. She was gaining on him. He was swifter than she had thought, but she was catching up.

But then, rounding a corner, she came face to face with a large group of tourists. In the crowd, he was lost to her. Out of sight. In seconds, he would be gone completely. In her haste to follow him, she had to fight the crowd.

She sprinted across the street, dodging her way through the throngs. Where had he gone?

Katie stood for a moment, her breath coming in great gulps as she looked around for him.

There he was. She caught sight of him again and felt her heart thudding in her chest. She wanted to shout out his name, to check for that inadvertent reaction that would confirm she had the right guy. But she couldn't do that here. She didn't want him to know she was following him, until she caught him.

She started to run again, pushing through the swarms of tourists who were taking photographs. She was gasping for breath, but she had to keep going.

Now, she could see he was heading into the visitor's center, through the glass-fronted, curved building with its round logo on the wall outside.

Katie burst through the door and headed inside. There were a few people here, but at this hour, it wasn't as busy as the restaurant area. She guessed the center was closing soon. With the evening getting later, Dolan would be under more pressure to make his move.

Had he walked up the stairs? She ran up to the top of the stairs and looked along the hallway. No sign of him, but there was an exit up ahead. If he made it through that door, she would lose him completely.

Katie rushed up to the exit door at the back of the building. The door opened out onto a parking lot half-filled with buses and tour coaches. She paused, her chest heaving. There was nobody nearby. She didn't think he'd gone this way.

And then she turned back inside and spotted him, on the walkway opposite, heading toward the other exit door.

She hurried toward him, trying to brace herself for the moment when she would stand in front of him, when she would know for sure that she had caught the killer. She could feel her heart pounding.

It was time to take him down. She was close enough.

The icy air whipped around her, chilling her to the bone. She could hear her breath rasping in her throat as she barreled after him, her feet flying.

She was on him before he reached the stairs. She grabbed his arm and pulled it behind his back and held him firmly. She brought the gun up, ready.

"Don't move," she said through gritted teeth.

"What's this all about?" he asked in a horrified tone. He tensed in her grasp.

Katie stepped around him and looked at his face.

To her confusion, it wasn't the killer. She was looking at an ordinary man in his early thirties, with a neat haircut and a slight paunch. His features were surprisingly similar and his eye color identical. But now that she was face to face with him, she saw he was not the man they needed.

She'd just wasted precious minutes following the wrong lead.

Could she do nothing right on this case, Katie berated herself.

The man looked at her in uncomprehending shock. "What is this?" He sounded Canadian, and he sounded irate, as if he was shocked by how authorities behaved on this side of the border.

She let out a breath and lowered her weapon. A look of relief crossed his face.

"FBI," she explained. "We're looking for a suspect. You fit his description and seemed to be acting furtively. Apologies for the inconvenience," she added.

The man looked embarrassed. He replied, "I was looking for the restroom. It's my first time here, and I got lost."

"No problem," Katie said. "But you need to take care. There's a killer on the loose who may be on the hunt for someone similar looking. Please, go straight to your vehicle. Get to your lodgings or go home as soon as you can. Better use a restroom elsewhere.

He shook her hand, still looking a bit pale. "I will," he said.

She watched him walk away and headed back the way she had come. As she strode back to the tourist epicenter, she thought about the killer. Where had he gone? Was he gone at all? Or was he still waiting?

She'd made one mistake and wasted time tracking an innocent guy. With time running out, Katie knew she couldn't afford to make another.

The killer hadn't made any mistakes yet.

Thinking about that gave her an idea. Perhaps there was a way they could force his hand.

CHAPTER THIRTEEN

Dolan was hiding out in the men's restroom in the visitor's center. The center was warm and quiet. He'd bought a coffee and drunk it on the way in. Just like a regular tourist. He laughed inwardly, knowing they were on his trail. But he was ahead.

He felt exhilarated. He had a fresh plan now, a new objective. The voices in his head were quiet at last. He was free from their criticism.

He'd heard the police sirens and suspected that the police had learned about the murders. It was time to get moving. They'd be searching frantically for the wrong guy. The person he'd fooled them into thinking he was. He knew they weren't going to find him. Not yet. He was safe. For now.

He peered out through the gap in the door. Two cops were walking by. He heard the crackle of radios. They were looking alert and watchful. Seeing them made him feel more uneasy than he'd expected.

He saw one of them turn, looking back toward the restroom, and felt a moment of panic. Maybe they were going to search the restrooms. Maybe they already knew he was here. He felt a bead of sweat trickle down his back.

He thought quickly and decided he must hold his nerve. He was too far ahead of them to have to worry. And soon, he'd be further.

He had to wait it out.

Unaware that he was doing so, his hand crept down to his belt, where he kept his weapon. He gripped the knife's handle tightly and felt the cold steel against his palm.

The cold words in his mind began whispering.

He lowered his head and buried it in his hands, trying to ward off the return of the voices. He didn't want them back. They'd been quiet for the past hour. He'd been able to hold them at bay. He'd been able to silence them.

Now, with them whispering at him, he felt confused and uncertain. If the cops walked in on him here, he wasn't sure what he could do, because he was a nobody. Useless. A failure.

But they didn't.

Instead, he saw the guy he needed. A man who looked like him. Average height, sandy brown hair. Wearing a brown coat. He was heading down the corridor looking confused, but as he saw the restroom sign, he headed to it fast.

Dolan quickly retreated inside and made as if he was washing his hands.

He saw the guy come in. He didn't even look at Dolan. He headed straight for one of the stalls in a hurry, seeming anxious and flustered.

Dolan waited, heart pounding, but in a pleasurable way. He never felt more alive than at these moments. He knew one of the other stalls was occupied but he thought the timing would work.

Sure enough, a moment later, another man walked out of the stall on the far left. He headed out of the restrooms. Now Dolan and his new double were alone.

He walked quietly over to the closed door and waited outside. He heard the toilet flush. Then, a moment later, the door swung open.

The man inside gave a startled cry at being face to face with a stranger. It was the last sound he made. Dolan couldn't waste time. He didn't want anyone walking in on this. Not now.

He lunged into the stall and grabbed the guy round the neck. Strangulation would work best. He didn't want blood. He felt a thrill as the man's breath caught in his throat. He was struggling, but his efforts were focused on Dolan's fingers. He was wearing gloves and his fingers were strong.

He squeezed the man's neck and felt his body quivering. Increasing his grip, he pressed his fingers into the man's neck. Just in case, he kicked the door closed while he worked.

"Sorry, guy," he whispered. "Sorry to have to do this. I need you to get where I'm going. You don't mind, do you?"

The guy didn't reply. Of course, that was because he couldn't. He was struggling but Dolan kept his grip tight. He wanted it to be over quickly. He held him up and watched his eyes glaze over as he died. Then, he grabbed the man's wallet, which was lying on the floor, and took out a few bills.

Dolan yanked off the guy's coat and gloves and pulled off the hat. He quickly transferred everything over to himself.

He was the same height and the same build. The guy he'd just killed had a small paunch, but otherwise, close enough. He was good to go.

He walked out casually, leaving the dead guy in the stall on the floor. He pulled the door closed. He was feeling full of power. He could see the future. He had a plan. He had another life. A whole new one.

The first step of his plan had gone smoothly. Now, he had to be careful. He had to be clever. And above all, he had to be ruthless.

Feeling relaxed and confident, he headed out of the tourist center and bought a bus ticket to Ontario. He presented his new ID, noting that he was now Paul Feathers. Feathers. He liked the name. He liked the idea that he could be someone else. In prison, he'd only been Dolan. Dolan, Dolan. He hated his real name. It was what the voices called him, and in prison, they had become very loud.

He climbed onto the bus and chose a seat at the back. He closed his eyes, savoring the moment. He knew he would get where he needed to be. He could feel it.

Around him, he heard the murmur of voices and laughter. The sound washed over him. He didn't identify with it. Didn't want to know about the lives and emotions of the warmly wrapped tourists who shared this bus with him. They were not his target. He had no need of them now and could ignore them.

He settled back into his seat and relaxed. He breathed deeply. He was free.

"Do you want to purchase some refreshments?" the attendant asked.

He shook his head. "No," he said. "I'm not thirsty."

She gave him a polite smile and walked on.

He didn't have need of refreshments because Paul Feathers had considerately left him a bottle of water in his coat pocket. And a packet of peanuts. He ate them slowly, enjoying the saltiness.

The bus started up and drove across Whirlpool Bridge. The snow had stopped but the heavy clouds were still hanging low. He watched the river below.

The water was calm and deceptively still. But below the surface, there was a dangerous current. The river was full of rapids and waterfalls. He felt a kinship with it. He, too, looked like an ordinary guy. But below the surface, he too was deadly.

He wondered what it would be like to plunge over the edge. To be swept away by the power of the water. To be tumbled and tossed by the river. He reached down and felt the knife in his pocket. He smiled.

Watching the landscape roll by, he felt a sense of transcendence. There was no one to control him. No one to tell him what to do. He was the one with the power, who held life and death in his hands.

He knew where he was going and felt excited about it, deciding to get off the bus as soon as possible. Then, perhaps, he would hitch a ride. Canadians were generous, trusting folk. They wouldn't mind giving a stranger a ride. A likable, ordinary stranger. An average guy in every way with a nice, relatable name. Paul Feathers.

It was a good name. He looked forward to taking it on. He could be a nice guy. For a while.

He walked briskly toward the front of the bus. He'd get off here. He didn't mind walking. A couple sitting at the front of the bus smiled at him as he passed them, and he smiled back.

The bus slowed down. He got to the front door and stepped off. He'd made it. He was treading on Canadian soil, free and clear.

So far, everything was going perfectly. He couldn't wait for the next step of his journey.

CHAPTER FOURTEEN

Leblanc strode along the well-lit road, lined with restaurants and bars and small hotels. He'd started out thinking the killer could be anywhere. Now, he was frustrated that Dolan seemed to be nowhere. His search hadn't uncovered a thing.

He'd gone into the hotels and bars and talked to the bartenders and the clerks. Nobody had recognized the photo or seen the man. He hadn't checked in anywhere under that name.

At that moment, his phone rang.

"We've found the car. It's parked on Grove Avenue," Harkness said, sounding excited.

Leblanc checked his GPS. He was close to Grove Avenue.

"I'll be there in five," he said, and ran for it. Would the car lead them to Dolan? What would they find there?

Ahead of him, he saw the river. A snowplow had pushed the snow aside and created a wide path, making it easy to walk along the water's edge. The cold night air swept along the river, making him shiver. He turned onto the next road which led to Grove.

Would the car lead them to the killer? Leblanc hoped so. Perhaps he was even sheltering inside it. It wasn't impossible that he could do that. Grove Avenue was a few streets away from the main tourist area. He might have thought they wouldn't search that far.

As soon as he reached Grove Avenue, the blue flashing lights led him to the car he needed. The road was closed. He showed his badge and sprinted past.

There was a uniformed officer standing out front, guarding the scene. Harkness climbed out of the police car and walked with him to the SUV.

"I just got here. No idea if he's inside," he said.

Leblanc drew his gun, wishing he could see into the car's darkly tinted windows. He went cautiously over to the car and crouched down by the driver's side door.

There was no sign of anyone inside. No fog on the windows, he noticed. A person couldn't hide their body heat. That was a sure sign.

Stepping back, he saw a trail of footprints cutting through the snow, leading away from the car.

"He can't be inside," he said, disappointed.

He and Harkness stared at the white Toyota SUV. Impulsively, Leblanc tried the driver's door. To his surprise, it opened.

He let out a breath as he saw the car was unoccupied.

The interior was immaculate. Not a speck of dust anywhere. It looked like it was waiting to be driven to the car wash.

The seats were covered with dark gray cloth. The interior smelled of lemon disinfectant.

Then his gaze sharpened as he saw something in the cubbyhole between the seats.

Leblanc turned on his phone's flashlight to take a closer look.

His eyes widened as he realized what he was seeing. Neatly stored, were the owner's possessions. Dave Bradshaw's phone. His wallet. His passport. Even the car keys were neatly placed in that central console.

"What the hell is going on here?" Harkness said.

"I've got a bad feeling about this. A really bad feeling. If he's left the items here, it's because he doesn't need them. He was misleading us all along, like my partner suspected," Leblanc said, his voice hard.

"You mean?" Harkness asked.

"He wanted to keep us caught up in this search, looking for this car and this victim. Meanwhile, he's made other plans to get across the border." Leblanc thought again of what Katie had predicted. She'd wondered if he'd been planning to double-cross them. He'd done exactly that.

Reluctant admiration filled him at how accurately she'd read his intentions.

Leblanc looked at Harkness. Harkness lifted his radio.

"Let's not let him slip away this time," he said to Leblanc. Then, into his radio, he said, "Call the border guards. Alert the team. We're no longer looking for Dave Bradshaw, or for his vehicle. The suspect may already have taken on another identity. We need to look for anyone matching his physical description. If you're uncertain, hold the suspect and we'll get there to confirm it with fingerprints."

He disconnected. "Hopefully we can still stop him," he said.

"It may be too late," Leblanc warned. That empty car with the ID stored away was a bad sign.

At that moment, Harkness's phone started ringing. He looked down at it and frowned. He answered. With a feeling of doom, Leblanc saw his expression change.

Harkness disconnected the call. He stared at Leblanc grimly.

"A man's been murdered up at the visitor's center. A cleaner found him in a restroom."

Leblanc felt a cold fist tighten around his heart. They'd been unable to stop this. They had been too slow.

"Jump in." Harkness gestured to the police car. "Let's get to the scene and find out what went down."

Harkness turned on the siren and the car sped up the road. They accelerated on the main road, tires wailing. Leblanc felt angry beyond belief that Dolan had been able to act with such impunity, under their noses and in a heavily policed area. Stashed his old identity in the car, strolled over to the visitor's center, and pinpointed a new victim to be his ticket across the border.

Leblanc and Harkness stopped outside and jumped out. They raced into the visitor's center, carrying their guns. They maneuvered through the clusters of tourists.

Ahead was the sign to the restrooms. One of the cops was standing guard, turning people away, while another was stringing crime scene tape across the entrance.

They rushed past and headed inside, to where another cop was standing. He was next to a man in overalls who must be the cleaner. He looked pale and shocked.

"I - I just pushed the door open and there he was," the cleaner stammered.

"Take it easy. Please stand by the door and wait for Detective Harkness to speak to you," Leblanc said, in a stern voice.

The cleaner nodded and stepped back, looking relieved to be out of sight of the actual body.

Leblanc turned to look at the stall. The victim was lying on the floor, face up, with his head almost touching the toilet. His eyes were wide open. Pale blue eyes, he saw, feeling coldness inside him all over again.

"Do we have any ID on this guy? Anything at all?" he asked.

"He doesn't have anything on him," Harkness said, going through the victim's pockets. "No ID at all."

"Dolan's taken it. He's using it," Leblanc said heavily.

Harkness frowned. "You think he is going to get across the border?"

"I'm sure of it. That's why he was here." Leblanc stared at the victim's face.

They were too late. They'd been outpaced and outmaneuvered by an adversary who was as intelligent as he was evil.

Leblanc stood up and turned to the cleaner, who was standing by the doorway, still looking shaken.

"Did you see anyone come in here while you were cleaning?" He was trying to speak calmly, but it wasn't all that easy.

"No."

"Anyone go out?"

"Not that I saw. I was only here for a few minutes. We're two staff short today, and there was so much to do. I have been rushing back and forth all day. I didn't see anyone, I'm sorry."

"I'm sure he was very careful not to be seen," Leblanc said in resigned tones.

Harkness was still bending over the victim, going carefully through his pockets.

"I have something here," he said. "It's an old receipt. Not much use to us. A cash payment. But it's from Costco in Ontario. So we know that our victim is Canadian. He visited the States and was heading back home."

Leblanc nodded. This evidence confirmed his worst fears. The killer had taken all the necessary travel documents, and the Nexus card that would allow him to cross via the nearby Whirlpool Bridge. Most probably, Leblanc guessed, he had bought a bus ticket.

He was in Canada already. On the run and gaining.

Picking up the phone, he dialed Katie's number, wishing he had better news for her. He hoped that while speaking to her, they would come up with an idea of what they could do next.

CHAPTER FIFTEEN

Katie couldn't believe her eyes as she stared down at the corpse wedged into the toilet stall. She felt shocked, guilty, and distressed.

It was him. The man she'd followed because she'd thought he looked like Dolan. He'd been searching for the restroom, but Dolan had been waiting there, ready to pounce. Clearly, he'd also noticed the resemblance.

Katie felt sick. She wished now she'd done more than just warn the man to leave immediately. She should have given him a police escort until he was safely out of the area.

Seeing this lookalike man had given her an idea about trapping the killer, and she'd been about to get hold of Harkness to suggest that they should single out some of the police who resembled Dolan, put them in plainclothes, and station them in places exactly like this.

That had been her plan. But Dolan had moved too fast. She'd missed her chance and now this man had died. Bitter regret filled her.

She looked down at the victim's face. The body was sitting in the stall with its back to the wall. The head was slumped sideways, resting on the toilet. The victim's eyes were open.

His life had ended because Dolan was on the loose and he'd wanted to get across the border, and Katie felt sickened by all of it.

She turned away, not wanting to look at the face of the victim. But in her mind, she could see his pale blue eyes staring at the ceiling, his face frozen in a terminal expression of pain.

Leblanc was in the restroom, waiting by the door, looking worried. Beyond him, the police had arrived in force. They had the area well-covered. The CSI unit was already photographing the scene and taking fingerprints. It was all too little, too late, she thought. Dolan wasn't here anymore; he was long gone.

"You were right," Leblanc said, meeting her eyes. He looked as discouraged as she did. It didn't make her feel any better, though.

"I didn't think Dolan would attack so soon," she said in a low voice. "I thought we had more time."

"I know," Leblanc said.

"I just wish I'd been quicker." Self-blame filled her again.

"How could anyone have predicted he would do a switch like this?" Leblanc asked. "Anyone. Even you."

Katie shook her head. "I should have thought ahead of him, because he's clever, he's a planner, he clearly specializes in misdirection, and he's cold hearted. He doesn't hesitate to kill, whether he needs something, or whether someone's just in his way. Every minute he spends out of jail he's a danger. He'll kill as easily as he'll breathe."

Leblanc nodded. "Yes. I see that. And he's now squarely in our territory so it's one hundred percent our responsibility. The problem is, it's getting late, and he could have gone anywhere."

Katie stared at him grimly. She understood what he was saying, even if she didn't like it. The truth was that they couldn't hunt him down now, when it was already after nine p.m., and pitch dark. They would exhaust themselves and it might well be futile. They could wait until morning and start fresh. But that seemed unacceptable. How could they wait when he was on the loose?

"There will be police searching through the night. Roadblocks will be manned. It's all we can do now," Leblanc said.

Katie shook her head. The thought of abandoning the chase for an entire night filled her with fear.

"At the very least, we need to pick up his trail."

"He might need to rest up too," Leblanc argued. "He's been running and hiding since very early this morning. Even though he's an evil psychopath, he's also only human. Either he'll have to rest up, or else he'll push on, but he'll be exhausted and start making mistakes. Whichever scenario it is, we'll have an advantage we don't have now. I don't know what else to say or where else to go now. We'll be casting around blindly, wasting time and energy and resources."

"You're right," she said, thinking that she had to accept the fact that they were behind the killer. He'd already gotten over the border and he could be moving in any direction.

Katie was tired and spent. She was tired of the chase, tired of the lack of progress, tired of the danger that this criminal was inflicting on innocent people. But she didn't think she was exhausted enough to be able to rest.

"I don't think I'm going to be able to sleep," she said, looking at him.

"You need to eat, at least," he said, and gave her a reproving look. Then he repeated, "He's only human. He's going to get tired. He's going to make mistakes. And we'll pick him up."

His phone rang, and he turned away to answer it.

Katie looked over at Harkness who was also on his phone. She couldn't hear him, but she could see him nodding.

She walked outside the restroom. The exit door was nearby. Pacing toward it, Katie stared at the tour buses parked on the far side. There were buses coming and going over the border the whole time and her guess was he'd taken one.

Her next guess was that he wouldn't ride it for long. He'd know they were catching up so he would change his game. That's what he was doing. He was outthinking and outmaneuvering them with skill and cunning.

Leblanc headed out to join her, pocketing his phone.

"Let's get going and find a hotel," he said, as if forcing himself to say the difficult words out loud. "Harkness has said we can use one of the local unmarked cars. It's parked just five minutes away."

Katie and Leblanc walked to it without speaking, both wrapped in thought. She realized Leblanc was right. The earlier crowds were thinning out. On this bitterly cold night, Niagara Falls was settling down to sleep.

The car was parked on a point overlooking the river. It was a beautiful spot at any other time, but now it was deserted and dark.

Katie started up the car and they drove across the bridge behind a large bus filled with tourists. It was the last bus to leave from the now empty parking lot.

"If we're not going to continue tonight, let's contact Scott and get a progress report," Katie said. "We must do that, at least."

"I'll call him now," Leblanc said. He dialed Scott's number.

He answered straight away, his voice sharp.

"I understand things didn't go the way they should have at the Falls," he said.

"No," Katie replied unhappily. "He got away. He's killed again. Unidentified Canadian white male of similar age and appearance. The police are trying to track down who he is, but in the meantime, we're sure he's long gone on the Canadian side."

"That's frustrating," Scott said. "From my side, we've put what we can into place tonight. We've already begun a search of the entire province of Ontario. This will start tonight and proceed in full force tomorrow morning. We're going to make sure Dolan's picture is shared with every hotel, motel, restaurant, store, and fast-food outlet. Where necessary, we'll go door to door."

"Sounds good," Leblanc agreed.

"We'll also notify every police, fire, and medical station across the country. We are going to have the whole country looking for Dolan," Scott said confidently. "And we've set up a hotline so that any member of the public can report a sighting confidentially. We should soon find out the identity of the man he murdered in the restroom. As soon as we have that, it will give us more information."

Katie felt more hopeful knowing that Scott was doing all the right things.

When Scott disconnected the call, Katie saw they'd left the border behind them. Now they were driving through a large, open area, with nothing but forest and wilderness to the left and right.

"Maybe he'll want to get as far away from civilization as possible," Katie said. "I'm thinking about where we spend the night. How far north do we go? How far will he go?"

"I've been thinking about where he might be headed, too. He'll change his game plan, that's clear. But he won't have much time for long, not with the manhunt underway. We need to narrow down his options and make sure he doesn't have the time to plan."

"I'm thinking he'll want to get a car. He'll need to use a car for a while, anyway, to put some distance between him and the border."

"That's possible."

Leblanc was sounding tired, and Katie wondered if he too was feeling relentlessly stressed after this futile hunt. They weren't dealing with an ordinary criminal. Even for a serial killer, Dolan was exceptionally cunning.

With Katie driving fast, they had already passed by the town of Cambridge, and there were signs ahead for Guelph.

"We can't go further," Katie decided. "Let's find a motel in Guelph. And get something to eat."

Even though this felt like giving up, she realized it was the only solution left to them tonight. It was dark, late, and bitterly cold. It was not in her to walk away when the fight was still on, but they had no other choice.

Where would he get a car from, and how? Would he just grab one from a rest stop, like he had done? That would be more difficult, late at night. Especially if he was still looking for someone who resembled him physically. Although he might not do that, since they hadn't yet discovered the identity of his latest victim.

So perhaps he would just lay low for a while.

As she headed into the small, comfortable-looking motel, Katie reminded herself that since Dolan was such a careful planner, he was not running blindly. He hadn't shown any signs of panicking so far. He knew where he was going.

Rather than running blindly in his pursuit, they needed to refocus on the clues that would tell them where he was going. If they did, it might guide them to his whereabouts.

CHAPTER SIXTEEN

Leblanc headed up to his room, carrying the small backpack with the basic change of clothes and toothbrush he needed.

He opened the door to his room, wrapped in thought. What a day it had been. Frustrating, deadly, and demoralizing. It hadn't ended well. But it hadn't started well, either. In fact, it had been off kilter from the word go. Now that he was alone, with a surge of renewed anger and resentment, he found his thoughts returning to what had happened that morning, and Katie's strange behavior at the maximum-security prison.

She'd been hell-bent on going there from the moment she'd heard the name. She'd headed off on her own, and when he had caught up with her, she'd been speaking to another lifer who seemed to have nothing to do with Dolan. She'd been distracted and non-communicative after that. It had been like pulling teeth to get her to talk.

So what was all that about? What had she been up to?

He'd been thinking about it all day.

He'd seen how upset she'd been about the murders. He knew how much she'd cared about seeing Dolan behind bars. And yet, something had been strong enough to pull her focus away for that critical time.

And he couldn't stop asking himself: was there something she wasn't telling him?

If so, why not tell him? They were partners. Or were they? Leblanc didn't know what to think. It wasn't like Katie to be so secretive.

It just wasn't Katie.

He wondered what was so important to her, that she'd risk the success of a brand new case to see it done. He wished he knew what had happened in that prison, today.

And suddenly, Leblanc realized that he could find out.

After all, he was an investigator. His case partner was behaving oddly and going off her mandate. So maybe he should spend an hour or two investigating her. He was now certain that Katie was withholding something from him. The way she'd been talking to the lifer in the maximum-security unit had appeared furtive.

Feeling strangely ashamed of the secretive action he was taking, although not ashamed enough to stop what he had decided to do, Leblanc opened his laptop, called up the databases he needed, and went hunting all the way back into Katie Winter's past.

*

"Well, this is interesting," he murmured to himself, after an hour's intensive reading. Hunched at the small desk in the motel room, his back and neck felt sore and stiff. He'd barely moved from his position, staring at the laptop's bright screen.

Finally, he had found the case he needed.

Katie had a twin, Josie. Now that he saw the name in the police report, Leblanc remembered she'd mentioned it. And it hadn't been in a way that had encouraged further conversation, but rather in the kind of way that shut it down.

Josie had disappeared in a whitewater kayaking accident. The report was very detailed. The accident had occurred in a remote area of the river system. There had been an extensive search, but the body had never been found. And at the time, Charles Everton, a known serial killer wanted for his crimes, had been at large in the local area. No wonder she'd made a beeline for him as soon as she'd had a chance.

Leblanc blinked hard. He had to look away from the screen for a moment. Emotions collided within him.

On the one hand, he felt desperately sorry for Katie. He could imagine the pain and self-blame that a cold case like this would have caused her.

But on the other, he was furiously angry with her, and he felt outraged.

She hadn't told him! Hadn't told her own case partner about a critical fact that was taking her focus away from the case. And she hadn't even been honest with Scott and the team.

Had she been so anxious to take the case on, so that she could get into the prison where Everton was serving his sentence in the maximum-security unit? Leblanc hoped she hadn't, but now he wasn't sure.

Even if she hadn't intended to speak to him, Katie had ended up doing so and deviating from her mandate. Most likely she'd been probing him for information, to see if he would throw her a bone.

And he simply couldn't accept that she'd kept this to herself. Betrayal felt sharp and piercing, a knife in the heart. She'd detoured to follow her own agenda which was bad enough. But what was worse was that she hadn't trusted him.

Leblanc let out an enraged breath. Enough was enough, he decided. He should tell Scott. Her actions could have compromised the entire team.

Angry and upset, he picked up the phone and dialed.

It rang once, twice.

"Scott speaking," his unit boss said.

Leblanc took a deep breath. He knew what he needed to say.

But now that he was actually on the line, the words wouldn't come out.

Telling Scott suddenly felt like even more of a betrayal. He was rethinking his impulsive decision. And worse still, he was starting to realize his own hidden reasons for why he'd had such an intense reaction to this bombshell.

"Scott," he said. "Just wanted to let you know we've turned in. We're getting some rest in Guelph. We'll be on the road again first thing in the morning."

"Good. I'll let you know about any developments," Scott said. He sounded surprised that Leblanc would be bothering to call with such a routine update.

Leblanc disconnected the call. His face felt flushed.

He'd nearly ratted out his partner for keeping information from him. Telling on her after secretly researching her would have been a far deeper stab in the back. And worse still, the truth was that Leblanc was doing exactly the same.

He was not in the right. He was also at fault, because he, too, was keeping secrets from Katie that he hadn't told. Even though his secrets had nothing to do with the case and hadn't influenced his decision making, he surely should have explained his background to her by now?

Jumping to his feet, he paced the room anxiously, riding out the tumult of his thoughts and the memories that suddenly surged into his mind again.

He'd had a female investigation partner in Paris. Her name had been Cecile Roux. He'd worked with her for five years, and they had gotten very close.

Leblanc leaned against the wall, cupping his face in his hands as he remembered how close. The boundaries had blurred. They'd been lovers. But they had still been a damned good investigation team.

He would have asked her to marry him, but he hadn't wanted to compromise their work relationship, or provide a reason for the powers above to move them away from each other.

And then she'd died. Leblanc would always blame himself.

She'd been visiting a prison, getting information from a murderer. She'd called Leblanc, asking him to come over and take a look at the suspect. He'd just been leaving the station, on his way over to her, when the worst happened.

A riot had kicked off. Prisoners had broken out of their cells, briefly seized control, and attacked the guards. It was a bloody, brutal fight. The guards hadn't been careful enough. The suspect Cecile had been interviewing had managed to stab her. The makeshift blade had hit an artery and she'd bled out before they could rush her to hospital.

Leblanc had been destroyed by guilt. He should have been with her. They'd had a rule they always did prison visits together, but there had been a mountain of paperwork and he'd run behind. She'd left without him, and tragedy had struck.

He'd been responsible for gathering the information, assessing the situation and the risks, and making a decision. And in that moment, he'd made the wrong one.

That had partly been why Leblanc had stayed in Quebec and not returned to Paris. He hadn't wanted to go back to a city where every corner, every building, reminded him of his time with Cecile.

All the things he'd felt, the guilt, the regret, had become all the more acute. He'd needed time to work through it all. He'd needed time to feel the loss of his partner, his lover, his soulmate.

No wonder he'd felt so utterly conflicted when he'd seen Katie alone in that prison corridor, conversing with that dangerous lifer. Leblanc hadn't wanted to acknowledge it at the time, but it had brought all his guilt and pain boiling to the surface again.

They'd damn nearly broken their fragile partnership as a result and things still weren't right between them. Perhaps they would be better partnered up with other people, as she'd suggested so shockingly earlier that day.

He shook his head angrily.

He wasn't going to mention to Katie that he'd researched her. He was going to put this entire debacle aside and not think of it again. But he also didn't feel ready to confess his own past to her. It still felt too raw, too painful.

"Let's think of the future," Leblanc told himself grimly. "That's what matters. There's a case to solve, a murderer to catch, and if we can manage to work together like decent human beings tomorrow, we might just manage to get ahead of him."

CHAPTER SEVENTEEN

Paul Feathers. Dolan liked his new name. He found it intriguing and amusing. Sticking his thumb out as he stood alongside the highway, he thought he would enjoy being Paul. A simple, likable guy. Your friendly neighbor. A man who would stop to pick up a hitchhiker. Karma, right?

Karma.

That was just a bunch of hooey. Payback. Cause and effect. That's what it was. And Dolan, or rather, Paul, was about to cause some effect.

A car slowed, about two hundred yards ahead.

Feathers smiled.

"Going north?" he called. He felt a surge of anticipation and excitement.

C'mon, he thought. C'mon. Stop for me.

The car slowed even more, creeping in his direction. It was perfect.

And then the car took off, speeding past him.

With a curse, Dolan waved his thumb again, stepping into the snowy road.

Sure enough, another car slowed. It was a dirt-stained Pajero SUV. And this one actually stopped, bumping up onto the snowy sidewalk.

"Thanks," he told the driver, getting into the passenger seat.

It was a young woman. She was wearing a heavy jacket and tight pants and boots. The tight pants rang a bell in his mind. Horse pants. This woman was a horse rider. He glanced around the car, noticing bandages and liniment, leather straps and saddle pads.

She smiled. "You're welcome."

Feathers smiled back. "Good of you to stop on such a cold night. Where you headed?"

"Kawartha Lakes. I'm going back to work. It was my day off today."

"You're a horse rider, right?"

She laughed. "Yes, I am, and more. I manage a big barn just outside the town. The job comes with thirty horses, three dogs, and shed loads of worry."

He liked her laugh. She was more entertaining than he'd expected.
"What's your name?"
"Mandy," she said. "What's yours?"
"Paul. Paul Feathers."
"Nice to meet you, Paul," she said. She reached over, offering him a hand.
He shook it. "Nice to meet you, too, Mandy."
He was watching her hands, her arms. She was a strong woman, but it wouldn't take too much to overpower her. This was a reliable car. It would blend in. It was a vehicle that could handle the roads.
"You're hitchhiking in this weather?" she asked.
"Yeah, I was on my way to visit a client, but my car broke down, so I'm just hopping in a ride. I'm going to spend the night in a motel. I'll sort out the car in the morning."
"Yeah. Definitely best to get out of this cold," she agreed.
Dolan could feel the adrenaline pumping through his body. The thrill of the hunt. The trick was to keep it together and not show anything.
At that moment, Mandy's phone rang. She grabbed it up.
"Hey, Nolene. I'm on my way home right now. What? No. I'm not going to stop for donuts. It's freezing out here and I'm giving a guy a ride into town. I'll make it home in no time."
She paused.
"You're ten minutes behind me? Okay, I'll drive slow and wait for you to catch up. Then we can both stop for donuts."
She laughed. Cut the call.
"My work partner. She's also been out today."
Dolan felt his tension ebb. This was not the time. Not the car. The unexpected call had just narrowed the timeframe. He'd be followed too soon. As he made the decision, he saw a small town up ahead.
"You can drop me here," he said. "I've just had a message from my colleague. He's coming through to fetch me."
"Okay, sure!" Mandy pulled over and stopped. "You have a good evening. Stay warm!"
She'd never know how close she'd come, Dolan thought, as he got out of the car. He made sure to keep his face turned away from her, so that she wouldn't think twice of him, remembering him as a harmless nobody. Although he'd told her his name, and that had been careless.
He might need a new name soon.

He waved, shut the door, and stood watching as Mandy drove off. Then he started walking. There was a sign for a truck stop on the far side of town. He'd be able to get further, in a long-distance truck.

*

Three hours later, the big, shiny Peterbilt he'd hitched a ride with slowed down. Hunched in his seat, the driver spat out his chewing gum and frowned at the road. It was rutted, and some of the potholes were wide enough to swallow a truck and trailer.

Dolan turned around to look out of the back windows. His eyes were drawn to the electronic lights of the truck. In the dark, he could see their glow on the road behind him.

And ahead of him, at last, he saw more lights. A small town. North Bay. He sat up straighter.

"I'm not going much further," the trucker said. There was a question in his voice, as if he was wondering why Dolan had spent so long in his cab's passenger side.

"You can stop here," Dolan said suddenly, as the lights of the town came into view.

"Here?" the trucker questioned. He took a stick of beef jerky out of a packet and bit into it. He didn't offer Dolan any. He wouldn't have accepted it. He didn't want anything that had been in that truck's dirty cab, smelling of sweat and soiled fabric and old food.

"Yes."

"What's your business here in this place?" he asked. He sounded curious rather than suspicious.

"I used to live here," Dolan said. He could see the guy didn't believe him, from the quirk of his eyebrows. He knew this guy sure did think it was a big coincidence they'd just reached his old hometown.

"Okay," the trucker agreed. He pulled over to the side of the road and the Peterbilt came to a stop.

That was Dolan's signal. Dolan got out of the truck, and as he did so, he inhaled deeply. He caught the scent of the forest. The clean, sharp odor of pine.

He turned to look back at the trucker. The man was staring at his phone, punching the buttons.

Dolan turned and walked toward the lights of the small town.

He was back. It was time.

And then, immediately, he felt a presence. He couldn't see the figure, but he could feel the shape of the shadow.

"Dolan," the voice whispered. "Dolan, where are you?"

"Dolan, answer me," the voice whispered in his ear.

Dolan stood up straight. He turned in a circle. He knew where the voice was coming from. He could feel it.

"Dolan, we don't want you here," the voice said. "You should have kept away. You're nothing but trouble. Loser!"

He took a deep breath and exhaled slowly. Focusing on the voice, Dolan recognized it. The laugh was familiar.

It was the same laugh he'd heard when he was a kid.

Pushing the voice away, Dolan quickened his pace. He closed the distance between him and the town.

It's almost time, Dolan thought. He was back in his old world. He was ready to hunt.

As he reached the small town, he was surprised by how familiar it seemed. Even after so long, and late on a winter night, his memory was sparked by thousands of small details.

There were two gas stations, a small strip mall, a few restaurants. None of them were open.

The houses looked the same. They were long, low, one-story homes.

As Dolan walked toward the houses, his boots crunched on the frozen snow. There was a fresh, cold wind that smelled of the forest.

He turned down a side road and counted the houses. At the third one, he stopped.

Dolan stood at the foot of his old mailbox. He remembered it, its peeling paint, its rust-eaten frame. It was almost midnight, and the house was dark. It looked different now from when he had lived there. He had to admit, the new owners cared for it better than his family had done.

They'd spruced it up. He tipped his head admiringly as he saw the painted front door, the paved path, freshly cleared of snow, the clean windows.

He remembered living here, what it had been like. Being part of the small community. He remembered what it had felt like, to call this place home.

He'd hated it. Even then, he was different. The others had sensed the difference in him.

Remembering the careless neglect of the house when he used to live here, made Dolan smile. The new owners had changed a lot. But he hoped they hadn't changed the one thing he needed.

He wanted to do this quietly. He didn't want anyone to hear, or to attract any attention. The voices in his head had differing opinions, but he ignored them as he keyed in the code for the garage door.

He pressed the numbers, hearing the soft beeps. A moment passed. Perhaps they had changed the code, he thought, disappointed.

But then, with a squeak and a grind, the garage door rolled up.

He could see inside the garage, which was well-lit by fluorescent tubes. It was a neat garage.

There was a red toolbox, filled with tools and spare parts. There was a neatly organized workbench. Most importantly, there was a shiny SUV parked there.

Cautiously, Dolan stepped inside. He took a deep breath. He strode over to the SUV and stroked the hood gently with his fingertips. He had his ride.

But where would they have put the keys?

He searched the garage and checked the tool bench. He looked in the pockets of the jacket hanging on the back of a chair.

He was becoming increasingly desperate. Had they taken the keys into the house? They could have. He stared at the garage's back door that led through to the home. He didn't want to go through it. This was not the time for noise. He put his hand on the handle but then he lowered it again.

Dolan took a deep breath and exhaled slowly. He knew it had been a risk, coming here. But he was committed. He couldn't turn back. Not now. Think, he told himself. These were trusting people. No crime in this small town.

He realized he'd missed the most obvious place. He walked over to the SUV and looked inside it.

The keys were in the ignition.

Dolan grinned. He opened the car door. He'd done it. This was his passport to heading further north.

And then, from behind him, he sensed movement and heard the tread of approaching footsteps. His stomach clenched. He'd been too slow; he'd taken too long. Now, someone was coming.

CHAPTER EIGHTEEN

Hank's eyes snapped open. He looked at the clock. It was after midnight. His wife, Madison, was shaking his shoulder.

"Did you hear that?" she whispered.

"Hear what?" he asked, confused.

"There was a noise outside."

Hank sat up in bed and turned on the light. He listened. Outside, he heard the sound of snow against the bedroom window. He heard the moan of the wind, and the creak of the trees.

"What noise?" he asked impatiently.

"It sounded exactly like the garage door opening," she said.

"It can't be," he snapped at her. Nobody would try to burgle the garage on a night like this. Surely."

"It made that same squeaking noise," Madison insisted.

Hank sighed. He was going to get no peace now, he knew.

"I'll go look," he grumbled.

This would be a complete waste of time, he was sure. He didn't want to get out of bed. It was freezing cold outside. Most definitely, he didn't want to go outside into the nighttime cold to check on the garage door.

Hank cursed under his breath as he scrambled out of bed. He pulled on his boots and shrugged into his winter coat. As an afterthought, he pulled his phone out of the charging cable and took it along for some extra light.

Sleepily, he stomped through the house feeling resentful. Madison did this to get him back for snoring. He was convinced. He shouldn't even bother to go to the garage. He should just wait in the hall, and then return to the bedroom and say everything was fine.

But at that moment, in the silence of the house, Hank picked up a tiny sound from the direction of the garage.

Had Madison been right? Surely she couldn't be, because who would break in on such a night?

He stepped into the hall and opened the front door. It was as freezing outside as he'd expected, and he shivered as the wind hit him.

He stepped through the door and walked carefully across the thick snow toward the garage. It was dark. So cold his eyes were watering.

He drew in a shocked gasp. The garage door was wide open. Someone was in there, messing with their stuff, looking to steal tools or their new snow blower.

Or even the car, Hank realized, righteous anger surging inside him as he rushed up to the open door. Whoever this hobo or vandal was, he was going to give him a fast send-off.

As he reached the garage, he saw the guy was actually climbing inside the SUV. He saw him as he glanced back, looking guilty and worried. Too late, Hank thought. With an angry shout, he rushed the man.

He saw the brown-haired, pale-faced guy reach beneath his jacket. He saw a flash of light.

Hank saw the knife in the guy's hand and with a clench of fear, he knew he had to act now.

He should run, he thought. But then, he rethought. Nobody messed with his possessions. He'd been on the wrestling team in high school. He could get the knife away from this hobo in a flash.

Running forward, he rammed himself against the car door, slamming it closed. The door crunched shut on the man's wrist. He let out a cry of pain and dropped the knife. It clattered to the garage floor and Hank kicked it away.

But the guy came back fighting. He shoved the door open again, pushing Hank back. Exploding out of the car, he punched Hank in the face, hard. Hank rocked back, raw pain filling him.

Then the man lashed out with his foot and caught Hank on the kneecap. He staggered back, his head banging against the garage wall. His leg caught a shelf and tools cascaded down with a metallic clatter.

Hank felt the cold, hard concrete of the garage floor slam into his back. His head rang. His attacker stood over him, looking tall and strong, his eyes wild. He looked dangerous.

Then he attacked, punching and kicking at him. Hank rolled away, trying to block the blows with his arms.

Remembering his wrestling training as muscle memory finally returned, he managed to grab his attacker's foot and pulled, hard.

The man fell backward, gasping as the wind was knocked out of him. Hank used his advantage. He jumped to his feet. He kicked the brown-haired man hard, aiming for the face, but he rolled away and

Hank's blow glanced off his shoulder. He scrambled up, but Hank could see he was hurting.

Hank grabbed a tool from the floor and threw it at his attacker, aiming for his head. The man ducked, and it clattered off the garage wall.

But a moment later, Hank was on him, kicking him in the shins. The man kicked back, but Hank was on fire now, fueled by anger and adrenaline. He was a fighter. He had to protect his family, his home.

"Who the hell are you?" he snarled, kicking the guy. "Why are you trying to break into my house? Stealing my car? What the hell do you want?"

Hank grabbed the man's coat and pulled him close, then slammed a fist into his stomach. One more of those and he knew he'd go down.

And then, from behind him, he heard a terrified scream.

His wife's voice gave him a massive fright. He froze. He glanced around.

There was Madison. She'd come out, wrapped only in a heavy dressing gown and slippers. Her eyes were wide and terrified.

"Call the - " he began.

He never finished what he wanted to say.

Something heavy and metallic bashed him on the head, so hard and painfully that the world went instantly dim.

He heard strange, muttered words.

"Sorry, dude. I never wanted to hurt you. Why'd you even come out here?"

He slipped to his knees and then down onto the cold floor.

Blearily, Hank realized that his wife's distraction had allowed the robber to strike. That was what had happened. He'd been hit over the head. By his heaviest wrench, from the feel of it. His head was exploding with pain and his vision was blurred. It was too blurred for him to see clearly or to stand steadily. He felt dizzy. The world was spinning around him.

He wanted to tell his wife: Run.

But as she screamed again, he realized she was already doing that. Her screams receded. But where was the robber?

He was gone, Hank realized. He didn't seem to be in the garage. That meant the man had followed Madison and somehow, he had to get after them. He groped in his jacket for his phone but couldn't feel it there. It must have fallen out.

For a dizzying moment, Hank couldn't remember who he was or what he needed to do.

He then remembered. He needed to get out of the garage.

With a grunt of effort, he gathered all his strength and rolled toward the door, dragging himself along the floor. He saw the forest ahead of him, beyond the open door and across the road. The cold pinpricks of starlight shone through the green shadows.

He crawled out of the garage and into the cold winter night. His breath froze in little clouds. The world seemed to get heavier and heavier. He rolled over onto his back. He tried to sit up, but he couldn't. It was as if the world had become a leaden weight holding him down.

He lay on his back, looking up at the winter sky. The darkness of the sky was getting closer, pressing down. It was like a great wave, washing over him, dragging him down into a bottomless ocean. The chill was immense. It blanketed him, paralyzing.

He heard his wife's voice again, but this time, it was a cry of terror. Then silence. He wanted to call out to his wife, but he couldn't speak the words.

He wanted to move, but that was no longer possible.

He heard her scream once more before the blackness returned, and sucked him in.

CHAPTER NINETEEN

The hotel room felt claustrophobic and overly warm to Katie. How could she possibly sleep when she knew Dolan was out there, gaining ground with every hour that passed? He was a dangerous killing machine. She knew she should be able to predict him, but night had allowed him to get ahead. She imagined him moving, a stealthy shadow in the dark.

Where was he going? What was his goal? It was too early to know. She closed her eyes, but her mind was racing.

She could do nothing about Dolan now, Katie decided, knowing she needed rest. But as soon as she stopped worrying about Dolan, her mind veered back to what Everton had said, in that short time she'd spent with him in the chilly, restless maximum-security section.

"She's the one who begged me to save her. She's the one I never killed."

What did that mean? Had he left her alive? What had happened to Josie? Surely if she'd been alive, she would have found a way to get back home?

Unless Everton had taken her somewhere?

Katie sat up in bed, the sheets tangling around her. She shivered. Could Josie really still be alive? Could he really have kept her, somewhere?

No, surely not. Surely Everton would not have done such a thing. There was no reason for him to have spared her if he'd found her, and if he had spared her, she would have come home.

The arguments circled round and round in her mind.

Why had he said what he did? Was he just taunting her?

He'd seemed as if he'd meant the words, but Katie acknowledged that the short time she'd spent with him was not nearly enough for her to figure out how he sounded when he lied.

She needed to see the police file. Suddenly, Katie wanted to read through that file again, to go through every word. Now that she was with the FBI and had a background in investigation, she wanted to know where the holes in the case had been, what the investigators had missed out on.

What had been forgotten, or incorrectly recorded. Those things could be important.

Was it possible Josie was still alive, after all these years? She kept coming back to that unanswered, and unanswerable, question. Hope bloomed inside her even though she tried to suppress it and knew the feeling was dangerous.

Firmly, Katie told herself to stop going down this road. Of course it wasn't possible. Everton was a vicious killer. He would have followed his nature and the pattern he'd shown. If he'd discovered Josie, he would have killed her.

She opened her eyes, then sat up, blinking. They felt dry and sore. Scrubbing her fists over them, she told herself to have some control. The day had been exhausting, and she needed to focus. Tomorrow was likely to be a tough, demanding day and she had to be rested to do her job.

She lay back down on the pillows, but her eyes remained open, staring up at the ceiling.

How could she sleep, when all her memories might be wrong?

Suddenly, Everton's face was there, in front of her. He was smiling. Behind him, a white wasteland stretched away. Overhead, dark, bare branches linked, forming a cage.

"Are you looking for your sister?" he asked her conversationally.

"Yes," she said. "Please, tell me where she is. What did you do with her?"

"You should have seen her," he smiled, that creepy smile she remembered so well. "She begged me to let her live. I felt so sorry for her. She was so young."

"Where is she now?" Katie insisted.

He laughed. "Do you think I'd tell you?"

"Did you let her go?"

He shook his head, still grinning at her as if they shared a private joke. "She's still here. She's always here."

She glanced around, trying to see her sister, but the white landscape was empty, bare. She couldn't see anyone.

She stared at Everton. "Where is she?" she demanded.

He gazed at her knowingly. "You'll find her when the time is right."

"Let me go to her," she begged. "Please. I need to find her."

She looked around at the white, featureless ground. The branches of the trees hung darkly around her, but now there was snow, blustery and thick, falling down on her. She could see nothing. The snow was so thick and relentless that it was hard to breathe. She tried to shake it off her skin, her face, her eyes, but it was everywhere. It was unstoppable. He was coming for her, too, in the snow.

She felt hands on her, grabbing her, dragging her away. Her sister was screaming.

Everton was waiting. She saw him looming ahead. She struggled, trying to avoid him, trying to move out of his way, but the snow was tumbling her directly toward him.

"No!" she screamed, fighting as hard as she could against the thick, soft wall of snow. "Please!" she pleaded.

Then, suddenly, she was back in bed, grasping at the sheets as if she was still trying to push him away.

Her heart was hammering, and she was drenched in cold sweat.

She lay back, trying to calm down after that weird, intense nightmare. But it had awakened images in her mind that wouldn't let her rest. The dream had been so vivid. The white wasteland, redolent of snow and ice and death. The bare branches of trees like skeletal fingers above her head.

At that moment, she jumped as her phone began ringing. Grabbing it, she saw it was Clark.

He was calling her at quarter to seven a.m., and if the early call hadn't clued her already, the urgency of his voice as she answered gave her the rest of the picture.

"Katie. We need to get going, urgently. It looks like he's struck again. There's been another murder in North Bay, Ontario."

"I'm on my way."

Katie jumped out of bed, filled with self-blame. The night had been the waste of time she thought it would be. He'd fled north and killed again. Far north. He was at least three hours ahead of them. That was strange. Why was he traveling so fast?

"Do you have any details?" she asked, switching her phone to speaker as she tugged on her clothes.

"It was at a home in the town. Neighbors called it in just now. Police are already on the scene and are setting up a search. I don't know the details, but I believe the crime happened in the early hours," he said.

"I'm on my way," she said.

She dressed quickly, grabbed her gun and car keys, and was out the door. She met Leblanc in the corridor. He looked as stressed as she did.

"Another one," he said.

"We shouldn't have slept," she snapped angrily.

He shrugged. "I barely slept."

"Likewise," she admitted.

Thanks to this debacle, the tension seemed to have worsened between them. Katie knew she felt angry and guilty that she hadn't done enough, and suspected he felt exactly the same.

She ran out to the car, Leblanc a few steps behind her.

Outside it was still dark, and there was snow on the ground. It was a clear, cold early morning, and stars were visible. The bitter wind blew snow across her windshield as she started the car and drove away.

She glanced at Leblanc, but he was staring straight ahead. She couldn't tell from his expression what he was thinking.

Katie drove as fast as she could, but the roads were slippery, and the snow was falling thickly again. It was starting to get light, but that only made the roads harder to see. Feeling frustrated, she knew she had to keep her speed down, even on the highway.

A sense of dread chilled her stomach. Someone was dead, and the killer had a massive lead on them. She was still more than a hundred miles away.

Driving in the silence, she was glad for the time to think about what had happened. To obsess about the case. As they drove north, Katie felt she was finally overcoming the residual exhaustion of her almost-sleepless night. She could feel her senses sharpening, her mind clearing.

Had Dolan changed his pattern, or was this a one-off?

This had been a murder at a home. Had he killed the homeowner? Like a home invasion? Why had he done such a thing? And how had he gotten that far? From what Scott had said, there had been no reports of stolen vehicles or any killings in between. If he'd hitched a ride, which he must have done, he must have left those people alive.

"Why that place?" she said aloud.

Leblanc shook his head. "It's a relatively small city, but it's on a highway junction. He might have been dropped off there if he hitched a ride. Other than that, it's an outdoor place. On a lake. Tourism is big there, but not at this time of year."

Katie frowned, trying to think of what would have motivated a serial killer to choose this place. To go all the way there, and then kill a local. What had his reasons been? Why that home?

As the miles sped by, Katie felt more and more convinced that if they didn't start to understand what was driving this killer to make these seemingly random decisions, they would never catch up with him.

She had to go where she didn't want to be. She needed to get inside his mind. And see what she found there.

CHAPTER TWENTY

The city of North Bay was not what Katie had been expecting. She'd expected it to be a gritty fishing town, but it was larger than she'd thought. She guessed there might have been a lot of recent development there, and she could see why. It was situated between forests and rivers, on the edge of the lake. Colorful signage proclaimed it as the 'gateway of the north.'

In town, she turned where the GPS directed her, and drove to a suburb bordering the forest, that looked to be an older part of the city. On both sides of the road, she could see the houses were small and cozy. The snow-covered woods in the background looked beautiful.

Ahead, Katie saw a home that had police tape blocking it off. A couple of officers were standing outside. There were a few onlookers, wrapped up warmly against the bitter chill, looking cold and scared.

Katie saw a coroner's van, and a pair of forensics officers on the scene.

She pulled up and got out. Immediately, a uniformed officer approached them. He eyed them suspiciously, and Katie showed him her badge.

"We're from the task force," she said, and he nodded.

"I'll take you to the scene."

They followed behind him.

"The victims were a married couple. Hank and Madison Brown. Crime seems to have occurred in the early hours. The husband was found outside the garage. He had a head injury, but it was probably exposure that killed him. The wife was stabbed to death inside the home." The officer shook his head. "We've never had anything like this happen before. Nothing like this, especially in winter when it's only locals here. The entire community is shaken to its core."

Katie gasped. A double murder? Was Dolan escalating his methods? He'd never done that before. Was it really his doing, she wondered suddenly. But it had to be. He'd been heading this way, although further north than they'd anticipated, and there was no other reason for such a vicious crime to have occurred. But it wasn't his usual modus operandi, and that meant they urgently needed to figure out why he'd done this.

"Anything missing from the house?" Katie asked, as they reached the double strand of crime scene tape, hoping for some clarity.

The officer nodded. "The garage was open, and their car is missing. It's a Honda SUV. We have the plates, and police have been notified province-wide. We put out an alert on it as soon as we realized what had happened. We've had no reports come in, though."

If it was stolen last night. Dolan could be hours away, in any direction.

Yet again, Katie felt confused. Why here? Why this little town? Why this particular house?

"Who are these people?" she asked, wondering if there was a connection between Dolan and his victims.

"They've lived here for about five years. Moved from Toronto, I believe, looking for a quieter life. She worked for a local insurance firm, and he was a builder."

That didn't ring any alarm bells.

"How did Dolan get into the garage?"

The officer shrugged. "That, we don't know. There's no sign of forced entry. I'm not sure if he overpowered them when they arrived home, or how he got in. Perhaps he just knocked on the door."

Katie exchanged a glance with Leblanc, seeing that he looked as puzzled as she felt.

"Who found the bodies?"

"A neighbor saw the garage door open when he left for work. He then saw Hank, dead and already half-frozen. He called us immediately. We found the wife inside the house."

This had to be the same killer, and he must have picked this town for a reason, but she was still no closer to understanding why. That was the key. Why here? Why this family?

"We haven't removed the bodies yet. They've only just finished up with photographing them and checking for any trace. So you can view them if you like."

"Let's have a look," she said.

She ducked under the tape and stepped forward, staring down at the husband. This was never an easy sight. Katie knew she had to put her feelings aside, subdue her horror at the crime, and think calmly about the logistics, the whys and hows.

Hank was a big, strong man. Peering down, she noticed cuts and contusions on his face and hands. He must have struggled with Dolan. Dolan was a vicious fighter, that they knew, but this man was bigger and stronger. Dolan hadn't overpowered him immediately.

The head wound looked deep. But what was interesting was that the police stated he'd died of exposure.

"I wonder if he intended to murder them at all. He's a very efficient killer," she said, remembering the bodies she'd seen so far. He had been brutal and remorseless.

The officer shrugged. "Well, he killed the wife."

Katie walked to the house, following the fluttering crime scene tape, to see what evidence lay here.

She walked into the house, catching a faint smell of blood. Her nerves and senses were on edge, and she moved forward.

The wife, Madison, was lying on her back. Her head was turned to the side, the eyes open, staring sightlessly at the wall. She must have been killed instantly. Her throat had been slit.

But looking closer, Katie noticed she was wearing a dressing gown and nightshirt. So she, at least, hadn't been coming home, but had been in bed when Dolan had arrived.

Katie walked outside again and looked at the footprints. They were confused, and partially covered by snow, but she thought she recognized the wife's prints, looking at the smooth treads of those fluffy slippers.

"It looks like Madison walked out. She walked to the garage. Then she came back, and I think he chased her inside," she told Leblanc in a low voice. He was stooped down, also closely examining the husband's wounds.

What did this mean? Katie knew it was important to piece together exactly what had happened.

"Dolan must have lured them outside, somehow. Maybe he wanted the car, or maybe he wanted to kill?" Leblanc suggested.

"I don't know if he did," she disagreed. Leblanc sighed impatiently.

"Why do you say that?" he asked. "You've been telling me what a dangerous killer he is. Why wouldn't he have wanted to kill, when there are now two dead bodies here?"

"Because he left the husband. I think the wife came out and saw him. He had to kill her because otherwise she would have sounded the alert and he'd have been caught. But his main reason for coming here couldn't have been to kill. He must have had another reason for choosing this house. It's on the outskirts of the city, sure, but it's in the middle of the row."

Leblanc considered her words.

"Agreed," he said reluctantly. "But then, we're back to not knowing. Which came first? Needing a car? Choosing this home?"

Katie felt the pressure bearing down on her remorselessly. She needed to think this through. Only then, only that way, would she be able to catch this man.

An idea occurred to her and she turned back to the personnel working at the scene.

"Is the husband wearing pajamas? Under his coat, I mean?" she asked the forensic officer.

He hesitated. "Is that important? I guess we can take a look."

He walked back to Hank's slumped body, knelt down and peeled back his coat. Underneath, the soft flannel fabric gave Katie the answer she needed.

"Yes," he said.

"So they were both in bed." Katie said thoughtfully. She felt as if the answer to the puzzle was waiting just beyond her grasp.

"We need to get going," Leblanc urged. "He's stolen a car. He has wheels."

Katie nodded. She knew that. She could feel the urgency, the fear, and the discord in the air. The killer was moving fast.

"Yes," she said. "We need to catch up, I agree."

But she didn't move. She stared at the prints again, trying to piece the puzzle together.

Leblanc fidgeted beside her. "Do we have any progress on a sighting of the car? Any information at all?" he asked the police officer.

The officer shook his head. "Not yet, but we're expecting it soon. We've got an APB out, and we're checking camera footage now, starting with the closest cameras on the highway, so we can see which direction he went."

But Katie didn't need the footage to predict that move. This killer - urgently, relentlessly, and inexplicably - was heading north.

"There must be something he wants. He's covering ground so fast. Where is he going?" she asked Leblanc.

Never mind catching up with Dolan himself. She realized she didn't need to do that. Rather, she needed to figure out his reasoning. Otherwise, they'd be wasting time.

"Let's start driving," she said. "Since he's been heading north, we can predict he'll keep going that way. But this time, will you drive?"

"Sure. Why?" Leblanc asked.

"I want to read through the case files again and get to know Dolan better. If we can't figure out why he's going this route, we're always going to be a step behind," Katie explained. "And when we lag behind, as we've already seen, the kills start adding up."

CHAPTER TWENTY ONE

Katie felt anxious and frustrated as they trudged away from the small, peaceful home that had so inexplicably become a crime scene. They were in a city known as the gateway to the north. It was on the edge of a huge, wild area and there were no leads on the car as of yet.

The wind was sharp and biting as they returned to the car. Every breath came with an icy chill.

They climbed into the car. Leblanc adjusted the driver's seat, pushing it back. Katie got into the passenger seat, turning the heater up as warm as it would go.

She did up her seatbelt, feeling the welcome heat blasting from the vents as Leblanc drove off.

As soon as Katie was settled in the car, she opened her laptop and began reading.

"What are you looking for?" Leblanc asked Katie as she stared at the case files on the laptop, wondering where she should start.

"I'm looking for the connection."

"Between what?"

"Between him and the latest victims. I'm sure there must be one."

If she could only find it.

As they drove north, Katie tried to put herself into the killer's mind. She tried to forget the snow, the cold, the darkness, and the tiredness that seemed to have overtaken her as the icy landscape scrolled by. She tried to think only of the killer as she looked through the case files.

She read through the files. Read more about Carl Dolan, starting with his recent kills. Before his attempt on Edith - the one that had gotten him arrested - there had been another, which Edith had mentioned to them. That had been the gas station owner that had fired Dolan. Reading the file, Katie realized that Dolan had researched him. Stalked him. And finally killed him brutally.

Now, it was time to find out if his earlier kills had followed the same pattern.

Six months earlier, Dolan had killed a woman who had been his landlady and who had given him notice. She had been kind and well liked in the community. He had known her, or researched her, well enough to be able to pounce as she'd headed out on her twice-weekly early morning walk.

Before that, there was a gap.

Katie wondered if that was because he hadn't needed to kill. But as she read through, case after case, she realized that all the victims were linked to him in some way. He'd known them all, through work or where he lived.

Carl Dolan was not just a serial killer. He was a planner.

"He's not killing randomly," Katie said.

"But he killed randomly recently. He killed random strangers who looked like him," Leblanc pointed out.

"Don't get me wrong. He'll kill a stranger if he needs to. But the earlier kills were connected to Dolan in some way. He's been targeting people with a link to him. We need to explore that. The problem is that he's never killed in such a northerly area before. I'm not sure why this is happening. It's out of the terrain he's covered in the past."

What was the link they were missing? Why was he fleeing north?

Katie stared out of the window, blinking her red, tired eyes.

"You're exhausted," Leblanc said. "You should get some sleep."

Katie shook her head. "I'm okay."

"You're not. I can see you're battling to stay awake. Did you sleep last night at all?"

Katie felt a flash of irritation, because his words sounded critical, rather than well-meaning.

"I'm not going to be useful to anyone if I'm asleep right now. So, let's just keep driving," Katie snapped at him.

Leblanc shrugged and turned his attention back to the road.

After she'd given her eyes a rest, Katie returned to her reading again. But as she probed into the case files, she didn't find the connection she was looking for.

Maybe it was that she was too tired. Maybe she was missing it, because her mind wasn't working properly. Maybe the connection was there, but she just couldn't see it.

"Hold on!" she said, so loud and suddenly that Leblanc swerved slightly.

"What?" he asked.

Katie felt excitement fill her. Finally, the elusive connection was there.

"The garage. That door was open. It wasn't tampered with. I know the police said the homeowners came outside and they must have done that because they heard the noise. But it's a remote door. It opens via a button or via a code. Could he have known the code? Known the house? I'm wondering if he might have lived there at some stage, when he was younger, perhaps."

Katie scrolled further back in the file. It wasn't the crimes she was interested now. It was Dolan's earlier life.

It wasn't there. His earlier life hadn't been covered in the file, so Katie had to access the databases and records to fill in the gaps.

Patiently, she scrolled through, waiting for the screen to refresh because the signal out here was patchy.

And as she read, she found out what she was looking for.

Carl Dolan had lived in North Bay, at that exact address, from the time he was eight years old until he was thirteen. It seemed the family had moved around a lot. Reading through the background document, Katie found that he'd stayed there with his father - now deceased - and his sister, Penny, who was five years older than him.

"That's how he knew the code. It was his old house," she told Leblanc.

"What?" He stared at her, looking stunned. "I can't believe you figured that out."

He sounded excited and intrigued. For a moment, Katie thought, they felt as close and in harmony as they had done on the previous case.

Then the car bumped over a pothole, and he hurriedly turned his focus to the road.

"I wonder if he expected to find some of his family there. His father moved away, but perhaps his sister might have stayed in the old family home for a while?" Katie asked out loud.

The thought chilled her. Locked away in the maximum-security prison, Dolan could not have known where they were. His arrival at this home could have been just to get a car, hoping the garage code was the same. But it could also have been to see if his family was there.

When Dolan went looking for people, it seemed to Katie that the outcome was never good.

"We need to find his sister. That might be why he's racing north like this. Penny Dolan could be in danger," she said.

"Get hold of Scott," Leblanc said. "He can trace Penny Dolan from the task force base, probably a lot faster than we can from the car."

Katie shoved her laptop aside and grabbed her phone. She dialed Scott, who picked up almost immediately.

"What's the news?" he asked.

"I found out something on the North Bay murders," Katie said. "Dolan lived at that exact address when he was younger. He stayed there with his father, who's since deceased, and his older sister, Penny. I was wondering if he might have gone back looking for Penny. Perhaps he thought he'd find her there. I have a bad feeling if he's looking for her."

"Give me a sec," Scott said. "I'll access the database straight away. Stay on the line."

While she waited, Katie looked out of the window, watching the road. They were headed on highway north, in the direction of a city called Temagami.

The snow had stopped, and now a glaring sun was rising, making the whiteness around them blinding.

"Okay, got it," Scott said a moment later. "She's still in the area, residing in a town called Ashburton. I'll send you the exact address. Ashburton is about forty miles north-west of North Bay so you should be fairly close to it by now."

"Thanks," Katie said gratefully.

But, as she was about to disconnect, she heard the radio in the operations office crackle again.

"Wait!" Scott shouted. "Hold on!"

Katie and Leblanc exchanged a glance. What was happening?

A moment later, Scott came on the line again, sounding excited.

"We've got a lead on the car," he told them. "It was spotted by a camera on Highway 11 going to Iroquois Falls. That was about an hour ago, so it's in that area. Police are already on their way. They have a vehicle and have organized a chopper as well. They can pick you up in a few minutes if you want."

"Okay," Katie said. "We've got two strong leads. And they're both urgent. Shall I go straight to Penny's place, in case he detoured there first, and you wait for the police chopper?"

"Sounds good," Leblanc said.

Suddenly, Katie thought, the investigation felt as if it had speeded up. They now had two directions that might give results. And more than that, she had an insight into his mind. She felt she knew more about who Dolan really was. Slowly, a pattern was emerging.

CHAPTER TWENTY TWO

Leblanc stood on the quiet side road where Katie had dropped him. Turning one way, he could see her taillights retreating into the whiteness as she headed for Ashburton. Turning the other way, he could see the shape of the police helicopter, a black dot against the low, dazzling sun.

In a moment he heard the thrumming of its blades.

It neared him, hovered, and then landed on the blacktop. Snow flurried up as the blades slowed.

The officer held out a hand for him to step into the chopper.

"You were lucky. We were in the area," the pilot said, as they took off again. "We just got the call."

"How long will it take us to get there?" Leblanc asked. "And where exactly was the car spotted?"

"Let me show you on the map."

He passed Leblanc a pair of headphones. Quickly he fastened his seatbelt.

He felt hopeful as the helicopter took off. Slowly, inexorably, they were catching up with this crafty killer. Leblanc knew that they had a chance to catch him this time. As he listened to the pilot communicating with the control center, he looked out of the window. They were flying over a white, snowy land. It was nothing but fields and forest, with a few ribbon-like roads snaking through. He saw a few small towns, a few larger ones, but there was no sign of major traffic.

"Here. Take a look."

Looking down at the map, Leblanc saw that Iroquois Falls was about half an hour away, as the helicopter flew.

Leblanc took a long breath. This was it. Finally, they were closing in on Dolan. But he knew the hunt was far from over. He had a lead on them, he was highly intelligent, and Leblanc knew that he would most likely be assuming he was going to be chased.

He needed to spend this time outthinking him. If the net was closing in on him, how could Leblanc work out where he would go?

He stared down at the map, translating the faint road lines and contour marks into the real life, snowy landscape, while thinking ahead, based on what he had learned from Katie's research. Get into his mind, Katie had said.

As Leblanc put himself in Dolan's shoes, he came up with a workable plan.

*

A little over twenty minutes later, as the helicopter touched down on a snow-covered landing pad in Iroquois Falls, Leblanc got out and walked over to join his hastily assembled new team.

There were eight police officers from the local force. Four police vehicles were waiting for them, ready to begin the massive search of the town and surroundings.

"What's the strategy?" the lead officer asked Leblanc.

"The car was sighted half an hour ago. So our first job is to calculate how far he could possibly have gotten from that camera point in half an hour," Leblanc said. "I've made a rough circle on the map. You may know a lot more about the smaller side roads he could have taken. So once we have this, we have a cage for him. Our first job is to secure all the outer perimeters of the cage, with blocks on every road that he could possibly take."

The team nodded. Leblanc could see they agreed with his logic.

"Then, we start on the perimeter and work inward," he said. "We need to search the town, but my feeling is that he won't feel safe staying there, especially not if he comes across any of the roadblocks. He's too smart to be caught and will try and look to hide. So we'll be searching the surrounding areas, too. My feeling is that the perimeter represents our strongest chance, and that he might be hiding out in a farmhouse."

In the distance, Leblanc could see the vast, snowy space that stretched from the town. "He seeks out crowds to kill. But when he hides, he chooses to be alone. We search farmhouses, abandoned buildings, old cabins. We keep roadblocks in place, and then we work our way into the busier parts."

The officer looked surprised but nodded, and then he and Leblanc climbed into a police car.

"We'll take north," Leblanc decided. "The rest of you, split up among the other directions."

As they drove away, Leblanc saw the officer dividing the rest of the team into two groups. One group would set up roadblocks, the other would begin the search, starting with the outskirts, using cars and four-wheelers. Above them, the chopper blades whipped as it took to the air again to scan the whole way around the outer perimeter.

Eight people plus a helicopter was not a big number, but it was all that was available at such short notice in this remote town.

As Leblanc and the officer drove through the town, he saw that it looked bright and clean in the winter sunshine, its streets lined with sparkling white snow.

The radio crackled with dispatches from the team as they covered their area.

Once they'd driven through town, Leblanc observed that the road branched. The main road stretched ahead. But, to the right, there was a smaller road, old and potholed.

"Which way?" the officer asked.

As he automatically indicated the road ahead, Leblanc realized that he might be making a mistake. Dolan would not have picked this route, he thought. That was what Katie would have told him. He would be looking to outthink them, sneaky and evasive.

Abruptly, he realized he missed her presence. That didn't make sense. He was annoyed with her. Mistrustful of her. And yet, he wished that he was riding with her in the passenger seat, instead of the cop.

"Wait," he told the cop. "I've rethought. Let's see what's down that smaller road first."

The officer braked hurriedly and swerved right, heading down the potholed strip of tar.

"You think he went this way?" he asked. "This isn't a good road."

"He'll be smart," Leblanc told him. "He'll be looking to hide out somewhere we don't think he'll go."

He hoped he'd made the right decision, because with the state of this road, it was not going to be a fast drive.

The car slowed, and then began to bump and jolt over the potholes. The wheels skidded in a snowdrift. Leblanc caught his breath nervously. The last thing they needed was to get stuck in this remote, snowy and wooded area. That would really slow things down.

"You sure he's out here?" the officer asked, clearly thinking along the same lines.

"I'm not sure of anything," Leblanc said. "But I do feel it's worth investigating this road. Look, I can see faint tracks in the snow."

Now that the road had flattened out, he could see tire tracks here and there, half buried in the snow. So someone had recently used this route.

The radio crackled. "We've searched the old abandoned farm to the south," he heard one of the teams report. "Nothing there."

"Nothing here, either," another voice crackled.

The officer turned and stared at Leblanc and he saw many unspoken words in that gaze. Chief of which, Leblanc thought, was the strong possibility of getting stuck. This police car was not a high-riding SUV. As he thought that, he winced as a rock scraped the undercarriage.

The radio crackled again.

"We've found a house off the side road," a woman's voice said. "It looks abandoned. But we're going to check it first."

"No sign of him here," the other voice came over the air. "We're moving toward the old bridge. It's a long one, with no other exits, and a good spot for a trap. No sign of him there, either."

"Okay," the officer said, carefully maneuvering around a snowbank. "Here's something."

They pulled up at a wide farm gate which was pulled halfway closed, hanging off its hinges. The snow was churned up beside it. Beyond, Leblanc saw an ancient, wooden farmhouse with a tumbledown barn nearby.

The entire structure looked like it was ready to collapse in a fierce winter wind. It didn't look occupied at all.

But the snow was churned. Why would there be tire tracks leading to this sad, abandoned building?

Leblanc got out, shivering in the freezing wind, which felt even more biting after the blasting heat of the cop car. On a closer look the tracks were definitely fresh. He walked through the scraped-up snow and pushed the gate wide. It creaked open on its rusty hinges.

The car drove in, jolting over the packed snow, and Leblanc climbed in again as the car headed down the hill.

He looked where the tire tracks went. They went to the barn.

"Stop here. I think we proceed on foot now. We need to be careful," he warned.

Climbing out again, he made his way toward the barn, pacing slowly through the thick snow, feeling surprisingly vulnerable in the glaring morning light.

"I'm going to take a look inside," he said, gathering his courage. "Stay outside and cover me."

The officer nodded.

Leblanc headed to the barn, listening out for any sounds, checking around him every step of the way. The doorway was like a dark, gaping mouth. The window had been smashed in. The barn looked more derelict than the house.

He stepped inside and gasped.

There it was. The Honda SUV they'd been chasing. Parked close by the wall.

Grasping his gun, keeping low, Leblanc turned. Every instinct was on high alert. His senses prickled. If this was an ambush, he didn't intend to get caught.

The barn was cold and dark. The Honda SUV was the only spot of color and light inside. And it was empty enough to reassure Leblanc that there was nobody else there.

"I've found the car!" he called, once reassured there was no threat.

The car's windshield wasn't fogged up, so there was nobody inside.

How recently had Dolan fled?

He ran over to the car. Behind him, he heard the officer pounding to the barn.

Leblanc put his hand on the hood and felt the warmth of the engine.

This car had been left here recently and that meant Dolan was very close.

"Get backup here," Leblanc said. "Now."

"Will do." Sounding tense, the officer ran back to the patrol car.

Leblanc looked around, scanning the ground near the SUV.

There were footsteps in the dust. They were faint but discernible and they led outside to the left of the big, gaping doorway.

Carefully, Leblanc tracked them.

Outside, snow had obscured them. But, from the angle they had taken, he thought that the footsteps might lead to the farmhouse. So perhaps he'd hidden the car in the barn and then looked for shelter elsewhere. Somewhere warmer, although the farmhouse didn't exactly look hospitable. It seemed to have been unoccupied for years. There was a stable block further down the hill, so it might have been a small commercial farm that had failed.

Perhaps inside was more sheltered than it looked. And surely the guy had to rest sometime? Surely?

Drawing his gun, Leblanc paced toward the tumbledown farmhouse, a hundred yards away, wondering uneasily if Dolan was watching from inside.

CHAPTER TWENTY THREE

Katie sped along the winter-slick road, with light snow lashing at the windshield. The heater was going full blast, but for some reason, it only made the car feel even colder.

Right now, she was driving through a town called Rosefield. It looked just like so many other small towns in this sparsely populated area. It was made up of a few houses, and a couple of small businesses. There was a gas station, a general store.

Her radio crackled. It was Scott.

"We've obtained a cellphone number for Penny. That's the good news. The bad news is it's turned off. Also, we finally have an ID for the Niagara Falls victim. Paul Feathers is his name. I'll inform the local police he might be using that ID. We've had a few calls to the hotline from various places with people saying they've seen Dolan, but so far, all the places are too far away for him to have gotten there. They're probably false alarms but we're following up on them anyway."

Anxiety clenched her. Dolan could so easily have detoured to Ashburton, using his false ID if he was stopped, to do one of the important tasks on his checklist. Kill the sister. With her phone turned off, there was no way of knowing what she would find there until she arrived.

"I'll call in with a progress report," she told him.

"Let me know if you find anything," Scott said.

She drove on, the car swaying from side to side, bouncing over the deep potholes in the road. Despite the challenging drive, she was making good time. Ashburton was now only a few minutes away.

As she drove, she thought about Dolan again, analyzing what she had learned so far.

Dolan was smart. He had to be. He was smart enough to have killed multiple times and gotten away with it. He was smart enough to have avoided capture for so long. And smart enough to have broken out of a maximum-security jail.

She was certain of one thing. Carl Dolan had become the person he was, early in his life. And because of that, he might blame his family for having ended up in jail. That was why revenge might be uppermost in his mind.

If this was the case, she hoped she was in time to save Penny.

Gripping the wheel, Katie let out a tense breath. She was here at last. This was the small town where Penny now lived. There were only a few winding streets in it, and Penny lived at number five of what was optimistically called Main Street.

She stopped outside the house and jumped out. The cold lanced through her, taking her breath away.

Where was Penny?

Katie hurried up the steps and rapped on the white-painted front door. This town was so small and quiet it gave the impression nobody at all had been here in a long time. Yet the snow had been shoveled away from the front porch steps.

She waited. Then she heard footsteps.

The door opened and she stared at a woman who was indisputably Carl Dolan's sister. She was in her early thirties with brown hair, strong bone structure, and a lean build.

Relief flooded Katie as she stared into her eyes. They were ice blue too. Penny was alive and well so far, and that meant everything.

"Good morning?" Penny asked impatiently. "What can I do for you?"

Katie could see she didn't have the faintest idea who she was. She seemed in a hurry. Baking smells flooded out of the house, and she had her answer. Something in the oven was at a critical stage.

"I'm Katie Winter, FBI," Katie said. "I'm looking for Penny Dolan."

The woman glanced at her ID. "That's me. What's wrong?"

"It's about your brother, Carl," she said. Then, as the wind lashed her again, she asked, "Can I come in? And please, attend to your baking if you need to, before we talk."

Katie stepped into the hallway. She was inside the house, out of the cold. She breathed in the rich, sumptuous aroma as Penny indicated right, pointing Katie toward a tiny living room with two cream couches and a crackling fire.

She rushed on, into the kitchen.

Sitting down, Katie saw the small place was spotlessly clean. The wall was decorated with paintings of country scenes. It felt odd that the house was so normal. Penny's mindset was obviously different from Dolan's. He was an aberration, and that was the sad truth of it, she knew.

Penny returned, brushing her hands on her skirt.

"What about Carl?" Penny asked, frowning. "What's he done now? I thought he was in jail."

"He escaped," Katie said. To her surprise, Penny didn't look frightened. Rather, she looked sad.

"I feel so badly for him," she said.

"He's already committed multiple murders," Katie said, hearing the sharpness in her voice. Penny's eyes widened.

"I didn't know about that. I had no idea about any of this. I'm sorry if I'm saying the wrong things," she added.

"What do you know about him?" Katie asked. "Has he been in touch recently?"

Penny shook her head. "Not at all. He hasn't talked to me in a long time. Not for a good few years. If you're looking for him, I can't help you. I wish I could, but I have no idea where he could be."

"He broke out of prison. He murdered the occupants at your old house, where you used to live. He stole their car." Katie gave the background, wondering if Penny would understand she was in danger. But to her surprise she remained calm.

"I'm sorry. He's a killer, I know. I don't know what went wrong in his life. Maybe he was made that way. I feel so bad for the victims. But I'm not the same as him and I'm not in touch with him anymore."

"He could be trying to find you," Katie insisted, her voice urgent as she got to the point of the visit. "He has already committed a string of murders and he's visited one of the homes where he used to live."

Penny looked blank. "He has absolutely no reason to kill me. I was always good to him. I was his big sister. I protected him. Looked after him. In any case, even if he wanted to, he most probably couldn't find me. I've moved twice in the past two years because of my fiancé's work. He's in construction and works for a housing company. And I've changed phones twice too. Stories behind that, but nothing to do with Carl."

Katie nodded. Penny was right. She didn't see how Dolan, fresh out of jail, could find her without access to the latest police databases. She felt disappointed in a way, but also relieved that Penny would be safe. Perhaps he had never intended to come here and had other places to go. While she was here, though, she might learn more about him.

"What could have made him kill? What happened in his life?" she asked.

Penny shook her head. "I have no idea. I'm older than him and although I was always protective over him as the younger brother, we weren't close. I had already moved out when our dad remarried. I left home and got a job when I was seventeen."

"Your father remarried?" This was the first Katie had heard of this. This fact opened up more possibilities, for sure. Now there was more family involved than she'd first thought, and more complexity in Dolan's life.

"Yes. Our mother died when I was twelve. Dad was alone for a long time. He met someone else when I was in high school. I didn't get along with her. She was a very unpleasant person, as was her daughter, and I never really knew them her well. Since my dad died, I don't keep in touch at all."

"How did Carl take it when your father remarried?"

"I don't think he was happy. He didn't want a new stepmother."

This was the first sign Katie had of the person Dolan had been in his early years.

"Do you know where they moved when they left North Bay?"

"Somewhere further north in Ontario, I think. I never went there. I lost touch with all of them for a few years. I know Carl left home when he was seventeen because he wasn't happy. There was constant fighting and problems between him and his new family. He seemed to be a different person than he had been before. He kept in touch with me for a while after that. Then he just stopped. I never saw or heard from him again. Not until he was arrested."

"What's your stepmother's name?"

"Bella Jordan. Her daughter was Bernadine. I'm not sure if Bella ended up taking our family name or not."

"Do you know where she lives now?"

Penny shrugged. "I have no idea. I do know they moved after Dad died, but I don't know where."

Katie nodded. "Thank you," she said. She stood up. "Please, be careful. At least ask the police to keep an eye on you until he is arrested."

Penny shrugged. Katie had no idea if she would do this or not. At least she'd tried.

In terms of getting direct information, this visit had been a dead end. But she now knew something important that might be useful if Leblanc's hunt didn't get results.

She knew that Carl Dolan had more family. Family that, according to his sister, had caused a change for the worse in Dolan's personality and behavior.

Bella and Bernadine Jordan had lived further north and they might be the reason why Dolan was heading so purposefully in that direction. The only problem was that she had no idea where they were, and nothing more than two names to start the search.

CHAPTER TWENTY FOUR

Leblanc paced toward the farmhouse, feeling every nerve in his body tingling. The tumbledown building was filled with gaps in the old, rotted boards. It provided the perfect cover for someone to lay low and look out.

And aim a gun. Did Dolan have a gun? By now, he could easily have acquired one, Leblanc knew.

The hiss of his radio startled him, and he fumbled with it.

"In position." That was the voice of the other officer. "I'll watch the back. You go in through the front."

"Roger," Leblanc said. Flanking the farmhouse was a good plan.

Leblanc moved closer to the building. He could make out its outline ahead of him. There were gaps in the walls, and he could see patches of snow through them that had fallen down through the partially collapsed roof. Inside, he could hear the creaks and groans of the old farm's timbers, shifting in the wind.

He took a deep breath, then moved through the broken garden gateway. He was in the open and felt intensely vulnerable. He couldn't see anyone, but he knew someone had to be watching. He moved cautiously, scanning the area at every step.

When Leblanc reached the house he paused again, listening. It was silent.

He was beginning to wonder if Dolan was there at all.

He approached the front door, gun in hand, and knocked. From inside, he heard a floorboard creak. Then it was still.

He stepped onto the porch. The door was hanging off its hinges, which wailed as he pushed it open. He walked inside the doorway, senses alert.

It was a dark, dusty, empty cave.

The place had been ransacked. Freezing air whistled through the gaps in the boards. He shone his flashlight onto the floor. The dust was undisturbed.

There was no sign of life in here.

"I can't see anything here," he said into the radio. "Place looks deserted. Wherever he went, he didn't come in here."

He stepped back onto the porch, feeling the cold air hit him. He looked up and down the neglected road. It was eerily quiet. No traffic. No other people. No sign that anyone had been passing by. This abandoned place, flanked by forest, must be all the way at the end of the road.

How was this possible, he wondered in frustration. Carl Dolan had stashed his stolen vehicle here. That was the truth, without a doubt. And then he had seemingly disappeared into thin air. Where could he have gone?

Again, Leblanc thought: didn't he ever rest? He was only human. After being on the run so long he would have had to rest.

And then his eyes were drawn once again to that small, innocuous stable block, down the hill.

"He's down there!" he snapped into the radio. "It's the one place we never thought he'd be. The footsteps went to the farmhouse, but he must have doubled back. Get here. Get down the hill. He's there! He has to be."

Footsteps pounded through the snow as the other officer sprinted around the farmhouse, staring at the small building down the hill.

Leblanc headed there at a full run.

Stumbling and sliding, he sprinted down the hill. It was a steepening slope and he had to watch his footing because the snow was deep and treacherous, but his mind was fixed firmly on the stable block ahead of him. It was the only possible bolt hole still left.

As he came within gunshot range, he slowed. This was too risky. He didn't want to be shot as he rushed this guy, who had already proven to be so dangerous.

He began to move again, now silently, keeping low. He was getting closer to the stables. He could see the building clearly, now. It was bigger and more solid than it had looked from the top of the hill. Sheltered by the slope, this place had withstood the elements better.

But the window was filled with darkness. No light. No movements.

Had he already gone?

He reached the stables, and again he stopped outside, listening. No sound came from within.

Leblanc froze, just for a second, then rushed the main door. He threw his shoulder against it. It burst open at his touch, and he ran inside.

The stable block was deserted. There were four stalls, two on either side, separated by partitions that were weakened and rotting. There was no one inside and for a moment his heart sank in defeat.

But there was another door at the back. As his eyes adapted to the gloom, he saw it. There must be a back room.

He lifted his gun, then reached for the door with his free hand, pulled it open, and stepped inside.

As he did, he heard a strange rushing noise from above him.

He had only a moment to react as a huge steel bar crashed down toward him.

With a shocked gasp, he ducked out of the way but didn't manage to get clear in time. The bar slammed down on his ankle, and he felt excruciating pain lance through him.

Leblanc groaned as he hit the floor. Pain shot through the parts of his body not crushed by the steel bar.

Dolan was there. He could hear him. He could actually hear his retreating footsteps as he sprinted out the back door of this small stable block after successfully activating his booby trap.

Leblanc could feel the hatred boiling up inside him. He wanted to grab the steel bar and smash it down on Dolan's head. But he couldn't. Dolan had fled. And Leblanc was lying on the floor, with his ankle on fire.

"Quick!" he yelled, as he heard the officer approach the main door. "He's running out of the stables and down to the woods!"

Gritting his teeth against the pain, Leblanc dragged his foot from under the heavy bar. It was throbbing. He had no idea whether his ankle was broken, or just badly bruised.

"Did you see him?" Leblanc shouted.

The officer rushed up to him.

"I didn't see anything. I heard a crash from inside. Are you alright? What happened here?"

"The door was booby trapped," Leblanc gasped. "We almost got to him, but he fled just in time."

"Hell. Are you okay? We need medics."

Leblanc shook his head, bending to touch his ankle tentatively. It was agony. "We need to get him. He went that way. Around." He gestured toward the back of the stable block.

The officer stared at him, concerned, and then ran through the back room toward the bright light filtering in from the half-open door.

A few seconds later, he returned.

"There's a big forest at the back. I can see footprints heading in there, but they disappear in the undergrowth. It will be very difficult to chase him. The trees and undergrowth will hide his tracks."

Dolan had fled into the trees. That would make it impossible to track him easily, and now Leblanc's injury had stalled the chase. But he wasn't going to hold up the show. Hoping for the best, Leblanc stood up.

His leg almost gave out. Pain seared through his bruised muscles. But the leg was not broken. He could put weight on it. He took a tentative, limping step.

"We need to try and chase him. To follow the tracks as far as we can."

"What about you?" The officer moved closer so Leblanc could lean on his shoulder.

"I'll be okay. You go ahead." He transferred his weight to the wall.

The other officer nodded and ran outside.

Leblanc started after him. He set his leg down on the ground and tried to push himself off with the other leg. It was a painful, slow process. He gritted his teeth and kept moving forward, one painful step after another.

He couldn't move very quickly at all. And he knew Dolan would be faster.

"He's gone!" he heard the officer call, and this time he winced with a pain that was only partially from his leg.

"He got away," Leblanc shook his head. "He was there, right there in front of me, and I let him evade me. This is unforgivable."

"Don't do this to yourself," the officer said. "We can still catch him. We know he is on foot now. He has no other vehicle at this time. He can't go far."

Leblanc felt totally demoralized. They had been so close. If Dolan hadn't set a trap, they would have caught up. Leblanc would have been able to shoot.

He'd never expected this man to set a trap. It had almost caused a serious injury, and it had been enough to allow him to escape.

Next time, Leblanc knew, he would learn from his mistake and not underestimate his adversary.

He pulled out his radio.

"Get as many officers here as possible. Encircle the forest. Roadblock the streets leading out. This is a priority."

He winced, putting his foot on the ground again and feeling pain jolt up. Injured now, he would be useless in this search. His only recourse was to retreat and regroup with Katie. If Dolan slipped through the net, then both of them could figure out where he would have gone.

CHAPTER TWENTY FIVE

Penny had been a dead end, but – to mix her metaphors – there had been some light at the end of the tunnel, Katie thought, as she drove north again.

She'd seemed reluctant to accept police protection and she hadn't seen her brother for years, but she'd provided new information on Dolan's family. She'd filled in a piece of the puzzle that had been missing until now, and Katie hoped it would be useful.

Ahead of her, she saw the signboard for Coldhaven, the town that she and Leblanc had decided on as the meeting point. Leblanc had suggested they go to the coffee shop opposite the local police department.

Coldhaven was a small town, one she had never heard of before, one of the multitudes of small places sheltering in the vastness of northern Canada. The streets were empty except for the snow being driven by the wind into soft, drifting piles.

Ahead, she saw the rendezvous point. It was the only coffee shop in town. She parked outside and headed in, her feet sinking into the snow as the sunlight reflected its tiny, shimmering crystals.

A rush of coffee and pastry-scented warmth embraced her as she stepped inside. The place was tiny, with only five tables. One other table was occupied, by an elderly man who was reading.

Leblanc was waiting for her there at the back of the coffee shop.

"I found out that Dolan has a stepmother and stepsister," Katie said excitedly. "Bella and Bernadine Jordan."

To her concern, as she neared him, she saw that his leg was up on the leather-covered booth where he was sitting. He had a makeshift ice pack covering his ankle.

"What happened?" she said, forgetting about telling him more and instead feeling stressed as she rushed over to him.

"He booby trapped a door," Leblanc admitted. There was an untouched cup of coffee in front of him.

"A door? What door? You mean you traced him?" She'd been so intent on her driving she hadn't had a chance to speak to him for longer than it took to set up the rendezvous.

"Yes. We found the vehicle. He was hiding in an outbuilding on an abandoned farm near Iroquois Falls," Leblanc said.

"And then?" Katie's eyes widened. She simply couldn't believe that they had come so close.

"Dolan planted a trap in the back room," Leblanc admitted. "It fell on my leg, and nearly crushed it, but I managed to get out of the way in time. We chased him, but he disappeared into the woods."

Katie shook her head. "That must hurt," she said, feeling a powerful blend of sympathy and frustration. She wasn't only talking about the injury, but Leblanc took her literally.

"It's not so bad, really." He shrugged, "It won't stop me."

She could see that he was still in tremendous pain.

"Can we get you a doctor? I can call one."

"It's just a bruise. I've wrapped it up and it's already getting better."

"Why are you here? Shouldn't you be setting up a manhunt on site?" she then asked, feeling concerned.

"There is a manhunt under way. But he escaped into a forest. There are farms, cabins, shacks all around the forest and it is bordered by two crossroads to the north. There are eight police on site now, and a helicopter, but it's a drop in the ocean compared to what we need. I think he's already gone. I've just been on the phone with Scott, organizing roadblocks further out in all directions."

Katie felt crushed by defeat.

"You were so close! Couldn't you have done things differently?"

Even as she spoke it, she knew it was an unfair question. But she was sleep deprived and frantic and her past and present seemed to be colliding in her mind, leaving her in a world of pain.

Katie could see that Leblanc was angry. She wished she'd kept her mouth shut. Now the words were out, and she couldn't get them back, and she saw Leblanc glower at her, duly triggered by her criticism.

"Are you telling me that you would have done it better?" he asked. Suddenly, it seemed to her that the atmosphere surrounding them had darkened.

"No. I'm not saying that," she began, but he wasn't listening.

"I was in charge. I had to make decisions. I've done this before. I know what I'm doing," he said, in a voice that was low but still tightly controlled.

She was caught by his eyes, as they burned into her, by their intensity, by the pain she saw within them, and she was overwhelmed.

"I didn't mean to criticize you," Katie said, feeling abashed and trying to smooth things over. "Really. I was upset by the news, that's all. I'm sorry."

"I did my best!" he said. "I thought I had him this time. I didn't realize that he would be ready for me. It was only me and one other officer. There was a massive area to cover. Resources were limited. We found where he was. We just couldn't hold him."

"I'm sorry," she said, shaking her head. "I'm really sorry." She meant the apology. But it was too late. She'd made him too angry.

His eyes became hard, and his voice was cold as he spoke.

"It's so ridiculous that you're trying to make me feel guilty," Leblanc said, "for almost getting killed. Perhaps we would not have ended up in this situation if both of us were equally invested in the case from the start."

Katie felt a pang of guilt, swiftly followed by anger.

"What the hell do you mean?" she shot back defensively.

"I believe you have been pursuing a personal agenda, and you are letting it undermine this case."

Katie felt her anger rising up inside her. His words were too sharp, too cutting. Far too accurate. She couldn't take the truth of them.

"How can you say that?"

"I know why you went to speak to Everton," Leblanc blasted her.

Katie felt as if he had thrown a bucket of cold water in her face. "You don't know anything!" she snapped. But she was on the defensive.

"He had nothing to do with the case, or Dolan. But everything to do with your sister. I looked it up! I know what happened. You went completely off your mandate," he accused.

Katie couldn't believe what she was hearing. She was overwhelmed.

"What do you know? Did you check up on me? I didn't need your permission to question Everton! Did you honestly go behind my back and investigate my past? That's unacceptable!"

"The information is available. It's on record. In the archives and in the public domain. It wasn't a secret. Of course I checked. It was an obvious time to search. I wanted to get to the bottom of the case. You were obsessed with Everton, and it cost us. I'm sorry to say it, but it's true."

Leblanc banged his fist on the table, causing the coffee and the cup to jostle and spill. Katie felt her mouth drop open.

"It did not cost us," she insisted. "I was obsessed by the danger Dolan presented. And yes, my experience with Everton taught me how deadly an escaped serial killer can be. But that's not the point. The point is that you, my case partner, went behind my back and searched my file."

"You were too focused on Everton. It was all about you. I just wanted to know if there is some kind of personal agenda behind all this. And there was!"

Katie was stunned by his accusations. She felt guilt and anger rising in her.

"That's not true! I spoke to him for a few minutes down in the cells, and only after concluding my other interviews."

"But your priorities have changed," Leblanc countered. "You are no longer invested in this case. I can see that."

"What?" Katie retorted incredulously. "This has nothing to do with my sister. I have never let my emotions get in the way of a case. I can't believe you would say that to me!"

"You deviated from your mandate. That is wrong."

Katie felt heat climbing up her neck as anger rose within her.

"How dare you?" she said, her voice low and angry.

"I can't believe you would accuse me. I can't believe you would go through my private files. Why don't you just go? And leave me alone?" she said.

"Why don't you?" he countered.

Unable to speak to him, or even look at him, a moment longer, she turned away and headed for the door.

She stomped across the quiet road. It was too cold to stay out. The cold was bone deep. It chilled her flesh and scoured her skin, making the blood pulse. Or maybe that was because of her argument. One that she didn't think could be resolved.

Katie banged her way into the police station.

She powered past the lobby and into the back office. Two detectives looked at her inquiringly.

Veering left into the smoking room, she found it was unoccupied, with a harsh tinge of smoke, and was very warm. This seemed like a good place to hide away.

She was shaking with anger, and rage was burning in her. It hurt. If Leblanc could do something like that to her, she didn't see how they could ever work together again. It was unacceptable!

But, as Katie sat and seethed, she felt her anger start to ebb. She was never one to hold a grudge, or a temper, for long. Even though she felt angry, violated, and betrayed, she couldn't help but acknowledge that Leblanc was right, in a way.

She'd let her personal feelings cloud her judgment.

Not only had she veered away from the investigation, if only for a few minutes, but she hadn't told him why. Case partners needed to trust each other, and she'd betrayed that.

Sighing, Katie decided that she couldn't get anything right today. Her head was aching.

This entire debacle had already done too much damage and she'd destroyed a partnership that had been solid and good. She needed to discuss this with him and fix things.

But there was no time, not when she needed to move forward with the case. The issue between her and Leblanc was now a personal problem. She couldn't allow it to derail her progress. When she'd made more headway, she would return to the coffee shop and talk things through.

In the meantime, Katie needed to urgently research the stepmother and stepsister who had been in Carl Dolan's life after his sister had left him. She was sure that this had a deep significance for Dolan. It might even have defined who he had become.

CHAPTER TWENTY SIX

Dolan smiled as he rode the red snowmobile across the snow-covered landscape. He was dressed in a heavy parka, fur boots, and a hat with ear flaps. All courtesy of a careless, trusting small-town resident beyond the woods who'd left his house unlocked. People were far too innocent in this part of the world. He even had a paper map folded in his pocket, in case the snowmobile's GPS stopped working.

The guy hadn't been home, so Dolan had been unable to thank him for the change of clothes, the food and supplies he had in his backpack, and of course, the snowmobile. But as a result of not being home, he was still alive. That had to count for something, right, Dolan thought, with cold amusement.

He thought back, with a thrill of anger, to that close encounter in the abandoned farmhouse. The dark-haired cop had been quick. Far too quick. Dolan was spooked by how fast he'd tracked him. He'd hoped to be able to hunker down there and regroup for longer, but instead, he'd decided to get going.

There was no doubt he'd been lucky to escape. The cop was good, and if he was still on the trail, he would have him tracked down in a matter of hours. He hoped the guy had been seriously injured in the trap he'd set. He needed him to be slowed down.

He needed to avoid the police, especially now that he was so close to escaping forever.

He could only do that by being cunning. That, he had learned a long time ago, but it had never been more important than now. His winding route through the woods had obscured his trail. Just as well they hadn't thought to bring dogs along on the search. But people didn't think. Not all the time and not like he did. All the dogs were down south at the airport, looking for drugs. Not out in the bitter cold, tracking his scent. That was the joy of this brutal part of the country, with its vast distances and scarce resources. Law enforcement often lagged far behind.

He'd seen the helicopter, far away. It had been following the roads, so he'd headed along the tracks and fields, taking the fastest route out into the wilderness.

Dolan glanced to his right, looking over at the shells and ruins of what must be an old mining town. There were many such abandoned towns out here, he'd learned. The 'boom and bust' towns that had only lasted as long as they'd fought the elements to mine.

For a moment he wondered if he should go over to it, if there might be anything there that could be useful to him but decided against it. It was likely to have been gutted over the years, and he needed to push ahead.

He raced away from the ruined town, feeling good. He was escaping. He was using his superior cunning to make his way to freedom. There was nothing that could stop him as he headed into Ontario's Unorganized North, a massive, sparsely populated area without any formal municipal government, located on the rugged terrain of the Canadian Shield.

The chill was becoming more bitter as the miles implacably rolled on. The landscape was dotted with frozen lakes and rivers, interspersed with knots of forest. He pulled the fur hat down over his head and flicked up the visor on his parka. The snow was swirling around him, and he was beginning to shiver.

He was on the last leg of the journey, and he was looking forward to his destination. The snowmobile rode smoothly over the frozen ground. The air was crisp and clear, and the view was wide. Miles and miles of uninhabited terrain lay in all directions.

He was riding the snowmobile away from his present, and into his past. Excitement filled him as he thought about what waited there. He'd held the anger in for years. Soon it would be time to unleash it.

The snowmobile was a powerful beast, and he was glad of it as he felt the cold of the subarctic air. He needed all the strength and power he could get.

The voices agreed. Out here, they were louder now, like he knew they would be.

"You're weak. You're useless. You're a coward. You're not like us. Not like we are. There's something wrong with you."

"You might as well let us take over, you know. We're going to anyway. You can't fight us. We're stronger than you."

Dolan smiled. Oh, he had no illusions. They were going to take over. He was looking forward to the moment when they did.

He just wanted to enjoy the ride. And he was on his way to make that happen. He knew the location, and with every mile, he was closer to reaching it.

He remembered what a stroke of luck he'd had in Northfields prison, when his cellmate had told him he'd known the secret that would allow Dolan to take his revenge.

For a while, his cellmate had been a builder in the north, constructing cabins in the wilderness, setting up off-grid systems for people who wanted to escape society. Although sometimes it wasn't only society they wanted to hide away from.

They'd spoken about that a lot, because every prisoner dreamed of escape, of evading the law forever. And where better to do it that in a wilderness so remote and poorly policed that you could live your entire life without the fear of being recaptured? Every person in Northfields wanted to escape and go off the grid. So it was a popular topic of conversation.

Dolan had been intrigued when his cellmate had told him about a project they'd done some years ago, to have a self-contained, off-grid cabin built in Ontario's far north. The customer didn't specify what she wanted the cabin to look like, but that it must be built to withstand the worst weather. It should be an impregnable fortress.

The builder had been vague on what the customer was running away from, but he was pretty sure it was a whole lot more than just being a recluse. But this was a cash job, and the money was worth the extra work that was involved in making the cabin impenetrable.

The cabin had to be built to withstand both the snow and the wind. Of course, the client wanted the electricity to be off-grid, and they had installed a wind turbine to power it. The builder had remembered the client well, as she'd been very beautiful and clearly wealthy, and he'd been curious about why she'd wanted to live all the way out there, on her own in such a remote and secure cabin.

He'd asked her and she'd stonewalled him. Then, he'd been so intrigued that he'd researched her name and found out she was a top model. Given that information, he'd concluded that she was probably hiding away from an abusive ex.

Dolan had been very interested to know the details about this client once he heard the background. And to know the location of the cabin once he heard the name.

He had suspected for a long while that this client had gone off the grid to hide away from him but hadn't ever thought he would be able to find out where.

He never would have, if not for the fact that a few years after doing the job, the cabin builder had been back home in New York state when he'd fought with his wife. He'd killed her. Shot her in a fury. And he'd ended up in Northfields maximum security.

There, Dolan had learned by chance about the job he'd done. And he'd found out exactly where this cabin was. He'd questioned the guy carefully because he knew it was very important to get this right.

Of course, he'd had to kill the guy after that. He might have talked, after Dolan had escaped. He knew he'd end up in solitary for it, but he reckoned a few more months would be worth it, and that the transfer might give him the chance he needed.

Dolan was a patient man. At last, his patience was going to be rewarded. He couldn't wait. He was going to savor this and make it slow. It wasn't often that revenge could be so perfect. He was going to make it that way.

He checked his coordinates, using the snowmobile's GPS. He was on the route and on track.

As he hummed over the snow, Dolan surveyed his route for the last time. He was nearly there. Just an hour or two away. Soon to confront the tormentor who had destroyed his life.

"What a surprise! Here I am again! You're looking shocked. Why is that, I wonder? Are you feeling scared? Well, I guess you have a right to be. You should be scared."

Playing and replaying in his mind what he might say, Dolan dug into the throttle and rode on.

CHAPTER TWENTY SEVEN

Katie sat alone at a desk in the back office of the police station. She didn't know where Leblanc was. She guessed he was avoiding her, and either working in the coffee shop, or heading out in one of the local police vehicles. Either way, she knew that they were going to have to fix things between them soon, but in the meantime, working alone was peaceful.

Now that she'd learned about the existence of Dolan's new family, his stepmother and stepsister, she felt obsessed about researching them.

Bella and Bernadine Jordan. Who were they, and what influence had they had on the young Dolan, once his older sister had moved away?

Logging in, feeling intrigued and hopeful that this might lead somewhere, she took a look at the various databases. The puzzle pieces were out there, she hoped. With the information she could gather, she hoped to fit them together.

Trawling the databases was slow, routine work. It always triggered impatience in Katie, but she knew there was simply no other way than going into the records and searching carefully. At least the systems weren't offline.

"Here we go," she murmured to herself, switching from one open window to another as she gathered the facts.

Bella Jordan had married Dolan's father when Dolan had been eleven. At the same time, his older sister had told her she'd moved out. So that would have been a big change for Dolan, and a couple of years later, the family had also relocated to a different town.

How old was Bernadine? Katie checked out that information and found that Bernadine was four years older than Dolan. She'd been fifteen at the time.

Katie wondered if the change in family circumstances might have triggered the change in Dolan's behavior.

"When did Dolan start showing signs of antisocial behavior?" she wondered.

His sister Penny hadn't mentioned that at all. She'd said she had protected him, but it hadn't sounded as if she'd tried to protect him from the law, but rather just been protective over him. But Penny had moved out of the home when Dolan had probably been twelve.

Katie looked back into Dolan's record to see when the problems had started, and if they did match up with the change in his family circumstances.

It was evident that Dolan's serious problems had begun when he was twelve. From having good grades, his marks had plummeted. He'd skipped school. He'd committed petty crimes in the neighborhood and in his own family home.

There was a long list of offenses, but it was one in particular that stunned Katie. At the age of fourteen, he got caught setting a fire in his stepsister Bernadine's bedroom.

"That might be significant," Katie said to herself.

Other problems had followed.

Katie noted his arrest for the vandalism of the school, then for the malicious destruction of property, for setting a fire that had destroyed his stepmother's clothes. She raised her eyebrows as she read that.

Even at a young age, Dolan seemed to have big issues with his new stepfamily. He'd been seriously angry at them. He'd wanted to cause damage to them in personal ways. Had that escalated, she wondered.

There had been other crimes, too. He'd stolen money from students and teachers, and later, he'd been involved in burglaries on his own street.

Even so, for a long while, Katie saw that he'd been able to hang onto his jobs and his residences. He'd managed to convince even people he worked with in an office job that he was a good, normal guy. Dolan had learned to keep his antisocial side well hidden. Perhaps he'd had practice in doing that as the years had gone by. At any rate, after being very troubled as a teen, he seemed to have learned to act normal and fit in with society by the time he left school.

So Dolan had cleverly controlled his image. He had pretended to be someone else, an ordinary man.

He hadn't, though. Under the veneer of normality, a brutal killer had been lurking. Katie read that he had committed his first murder at the age of twenty, although police had only traced it back to him later.

Leaning back in the chair and rubbing the back of her neck with one hand, Katie thought about this.

It was possible that the onset of adolescence had unleashed Dolan's monsters, but it was also possible that he'd suffered abuse or neglect at the hands of his stepmother and even his stepsister.

At eleven years old, he would have been vulnerable. Severe abuse could easily have contributed to what he'd become.

Now, Kate urgently needed to locate his stepfamily. Based on this new information, they were seriously at risk from him now.

But here was a curveball! Searching further into the database, looking for updated address details, Katie found out that Bernadine had been declared legally dead after being missing for a number of years.

"Now this is interesting," Katie said. "Legally dead?"

How was that possible, she wondered. With a killer in the family, it sure didn't seem like a coincidence.

Switching between the databases, she found that Bernadine had disappeared ten years ago at the age of twenty-four. Three years ago, she had been declared legally dead, but her body had never been found.

Katie read through the information. This was very significant, she thought.

Deciding she needed to put a face to the woman who'd been involved in such a mysterious sequence of events, she went into another database, to get an ID photo of her.

The woman she stared at had long, straight, dark hair. Her eyes were large and dark, framed by long lashes. Her face was oval-shaped, and her skin was a light tan. Her mouth was a wide shape and her lips looked full. However, Katie noted she had a determined chin, and a look about her that suggested she had a stubborn streak a mile wide.

A beautiful woman, Katie thought. There was no denying that.

Reading on, Katie found that Bernadine's most recent home had been set in the foothills outside of Toronto. It had been a listed historic home. There was a picture of it. It looked like a mansion to Katie. She wasn't sure what work Bernadine had done, but she must have earned well to buy such a gracious home.

But why would a beautiful, wealthy young woman who lived in luxury, suddenly vanish?

Her thoughts turned back to Josie's disappearance, and she shivered, wondering if Bernadine had suffered a similar fate.

In today's world, it was very rare for people to simply vanish. Tapping her fingers on the desk, Katie thought that all the evidence was pointing to Dolan having killed her.

What if she'd been the first of Dolan's victims, but her body had never been found?

That sounded like a strong reason to Katie.

"Yes, I think it's more likely that she could have been his first kill," Katie said to herself.

She wondered how much her mother, Bella, knew about the possible reasons for her daughter's disappearance. Bella might know more. If there was another cause, which Katie doubted, then surely Bella would know? She needed to speak to Bella now to fill in the gaps, but also to warn her that she might be targeted next.

There was a phone number for Bella in the archives. Deciding that she couldn't wait, that this situation was now urgent, Katie called the number.

She frowned as she listened to it ring and ring.

Bella wasn't picking up, and that wasn't a good sign right now.

Feeling seriously worried, she checked Bella's current address details. Katie drew in a concerned breath as she saw that Bella now lived in a town called Moonbeam, which was a hundred miles north of Iroquois Falls.

That was exactly the direction Dolan was heading, powering up into the north. Dolan had fled his hiding place more than two hours ago and could already be there by now.

Katie stood up so suddenly her chair almost tipped over. She rushed across the road to the coffee shop, but saw with a sinking of her stomach, that Leblanc was no longer there. She didn't know where he had gone, but he'd taken the car.

She ran back to the police station, and into the station commander's office, where he was just finishing off on a call.

"I'm heading out to follow an urgent lead," she told him. "Can I sign out a car? And could I ask you to call the local police department in Moonbeam? There's a resident there who may be in danger."

The commander nodded. "Of course, Agent Winter. I'll organize it for you now. Give me the address and I'll liaise with the police. They may also take a while to get there, though. It's a very remote, small town."

If Bella was still alive, Katie needed to warn her urgently that a killer was headed her way.

With no time to spare, she was going to have to do it alone.

CHAPTER TWENTY EIGHT

An hour and a half later, Katie arrived in the small town of Moonbeam, Ontario. It was icy cold. The road was slippery with ice and the wind was tugging at her car, threatening to send it skidding off the blacktop.

She'd received a message from Scott as she'd been driving. A red snowmobile had been reported stolen from a farm near Iroquois Falls. Dolan had found transport and could easily have arrived out here. She hadn't heard back from the local police. In this remote area, she had no doubt they were thinly stretched.

At the crossroads was Dujardin Street, where Bella's house was situated.

She turned right, and found herself approaching a small, quaint timber cottage flanked by maple trees. There was no sign of any police presence outside.

By now, any footprints would have been covered over by the swirling wind that was tugging at the bare trees. But when she climbed out of the car, she checked carefully for them in any case.

She could see nothing but the distressed, windblown snow, meaning he might have been and gone already. At any rate, there was no sign of a red snowmobile anywhere she could see.

Katie got out of her car and strode up to the front door, her feet sinking into the coldness. She stepped through the piled snow to the front door and rang the bell. For several moments there was no answer. Then she spun to face the window as she saw a curtain move to the left of the door.

Why wasn't she coming to the door? Was she fearful of who might be outside?

Or was someone else moving that curtain, Katie wondered, with a twist of her stomach.

"Mrs. Jordan?" Katie called out. "Are you there? It's urgent."

After a pause, the curtain was pulled back again, and the window opened a crack.

"I can't open the front door. Come round the back," a voice called.

Katie plowed around the side of the house, and up a small slope to the higher, more sheltered side of the home. Here, a path had been dug to the back door and Bella Jordan was standing there, waiting.

Tall and slender and probably in her early sixties, the dark-haired woman was still regally attractive. She could see where Bernadine had gotten her looks from.

But even though she was beautiful, Mrs. Jordan did not appear welcoming. She stared at Katie suspiciously, tugging her parka tightly around her.

"Who are you, and why are you here?" she demanded rudely. "Are you police?"

Katie reminded herself that the woman already knew her own stepson was a killer. She was on the defensive. That was noteworthy. Was there a reason for her to be defensive? Did she feel guilty about how she'd treated Dolan? She certainly didn't give the first impression of being a kind or caring person.

"FBI," she said. "I'm Agent Katie Winter. I need to talk to you about your stepson. I'm here because he has escaped from prison."

She watched Bella carefully as she spoke. But Bella's expression didn't change.

"Is that so? I haven't spoken to Carl for many years," she said.

She didn't seem afraid. Katie didn't know if that was a good or a bad thing. She might be in denial. At any rate, her reaction wasn't what Katie had expected.

"Since he escaped, he's committed more murders, and he's at large in this wider area. I suspect that he might be going to target you."

Bella's expression changed. It became a mixture of fear, anger, and anticipation.

"Why me?" she demanded, her gaze flicking over Katie's face. Katie thought the words sounded like more of a challenge than a question.

"He already stopped by his old family home in North Bay," Katie explained. "He stole a car from there and murdered the new homeowners."

Now Bella showed at least a trace of normal emotion.

"That's awful!" she said, her eyes wide in shock.

The wind blasted around the house, tugging Katie's hair and rippling the loosely packed snow that formed a thick layer over the backyard.

"Can I come in?" she asked, because it didn't look like Bella was going to invite her otherwise.

"Of course."

Bella turned and led the way inside, through a small but well-equipped kitchen, and into a neat lounge with a large window that overlooked a frozen lake beyond the town. Looking around, the lounge, Katie wondered how much this home reflected Bella's personality. It was surprisingly sterile, especially for the home of someone who was a mother and a widow.

It was elegantly furnished in modern gray and white, and on the walls were a few pieces of tasteful artwork, but nothing that looked particularly personal. There were no photographs in sight.

Katie took a seat on the sofa, and Bella sat down on a chair opposite her. She needed to get back to the main reason for her visit first, which was to ensure this woman's safety.

"Carl Dolan is a very dangerous killer. He probably knows where you are, and he might have a reason to target you," she explained.

Bella gazed at her incredulously. She crossed her legs and began swinging her right foot back and forth.

"I'm not afraid of him. He was an evil little boy, but that wasn't my doing. We didn't make him that way. I still cared for him." Her chin jutted defensively.

"You may be in danger. You need to be careful. Ideally, you should get police protection until we can capture and re-arrest Dolan. Would you be willing to do that?"

"Police protection?" She shook her head. "I don't want people around me night and day, bothering my privacy."

"Having police presence here would also make it easier to re-arrest him if he does come here," Katie tried. "So you'd be helping us."

Bella stared at her. "There's no reason for him to target me. I was always a responsible guardian. I did my job even though it wasn't easy."

"Innocent people have already died," Katie reminded her sternly.

"What do you want me to do?" Bella asked. "Do you want me to agree to be guarded? To be protected? Because I won't. I'll be fine."

Katie saw she wouldn't get anywhere with this. And in any case, police were a scarce resource here. But that statement paved the way for her to explore the family background. That was the second reason why she was here. She hoped Bella would be more willing to talk about this, even if it included the painful subject of her daughter's disappearance.

"I read that Dolan had problems that began when he was twelve," Katie said. "What do you think? Did he resent having a new family?"

Bella shrugged. "He was a difficult child. But I treated him fairly. If you are implying that he was abused, you should think again. He was not. He was a damaged child. We did our best to care for him regardless." She stared at Katie challengingly.

Katie sensed she was only going to come up against a wall of defiance with this line of questioning but decided to push on.

"What did your daughter think of his behavior?"

"The same as me, I guess." Bella's mouth shut firmly. That was clearly a line of conversation she didn't want to explore.

"I know Bernadine disappeared and has been declared dead. I'm very sorry about that. As a mother, that must have been tragic for you."

Bella nodded.

Katie felt confused by her lack of reaction. Even though her daughter had disappeared years ago, where was the pain and anguish she expected to see? The grief at the lack of answers? Had she walled it off in her mind, or what was going on here, she wondered, confused.

"When did you know she was missing?" she probed.

"I was called by her agency, who were battling to get hold of her."

"Her agency?"

"Bernadine worked as a model. She was very successful."

"Oh. Go on?" Katie now knew how Bernadine had afforded the sumptuous home.

"She hadn't been answering my calls for a few days. I went to her home before reporting her missing." Bella's voice was sad, but her face was hard. Too hard.

"Is there something you're not telling me?" Katie asked suddenly.

"What would that be?" Bella shot back. Katie felt even more suspicious.

"Did Carl Dolan contact her at all before she went missing?"

"How would I know that?"

Did Bella not even suspect Dolan might have murdered her daughter long ago? Suddenly, Katie thought of another possibility that fitted the facts, as well as Bella's reaction.

Was Bernadine still alive, but hiding away?

Katie knew she had only one chance to shock Bella out of her resistance and get the truth.

"Let's assume your daughter is still alive, but that she's chosen to hide away from Dolan. Off the grid, perhaps," Katie said sternly.

For the first time, Bella didn't meet her eyes. Her gaze slid away.

"If that is true, then she is in serious danger right now. Because Dolan is heading north. Far north. He's going as fast as he can, and he seems to have a plan. A destination in mind."

Now Bella looked both concerned and distressed. She was biting her lip hard. Katie's words had produced a shock effect.

"My daughter is in danger?" she echoed in a whisper.

"Please, help me here. Where is she?" Katie entreated her. "What happened? Why did she disappear all those years ago? If we can get to her before he does, we have a chance."

Bella now looked conflicted.

"She went into hiding," she said suddenly, the words bursting from her. "When she was younger, she was a headstrong girl. Strong willed. She clashed with Carl a lot. She saw the evil in him, and she opposed it. She – she did bully him. She wasn't nice to him, but nor was he to her. And then – when he started killing, we knew it was him. I'm not sure if you know, but his first victim was a girl who rejected him in high school. She was close to Bernadine. She mentioned the day before she was murdered that Dolan had been watching her. Then, Bernadine spotted Dolan a few weeks later, watching her in her own home. She knew what he was planning. I helped her get away. We knew she had to disappear immediately and without a trace. She hid away in hotels, moving from place to place, while she organized her retreat in the far north of Ontario where she thought she would be safe."

Katie felt shocked by this story. She could imagine the family's terror.

"Why did she stay there after he went to jail?" she asked.

Bella shrugged. "She was used to the life. She had disappeared, soon to be declared dead, and to return would have landed her in a world of trouble. She said she liked being a nobody and living off the grid. She grew used to being alone. I didn't speak to her often. I haven't for more than a year."

Now for the most important question.

"Where is she, Bella? I need to get to her as soon as possible."

Bella took a deep breath.

"Her cabin is on the shores of Missisa Lake. Near the south of the lake. I've never been there. I don't know more than that."

"Thank you," Katie said.

She stood up.

There was no time to lose. She needed to head far north, to find this freezing lake, and locate Bernadine's hideaway before Dolan got there. Quickly, she sent a message to Leblanc, telling him what she'd discovered. And then she ran for the car.

CHAPTER TWENTY NINE

Each breath of the chilling air, each mile that the snowmobile covered, brought Dolan closer to his goal.

He felt proud of his own focus and determination in getting there. He'd had obstacles thrown into his path, but nothing had stopped him. The years of sadism and torture had taught him well. They had turned him into a cold, emotionless creature with no reservations about killing. They'd shaped him into the person he was. And now, at last, it was payback time.

The real prize was so close. It would be a dream come true.

He'd imagined it so many times. What she would be like. How she would react. He had sworn that he would get his revenge on her. That one day she would pay.

He stopped the snowmobile and sat for a while in the icy air, breathing in the sharpness of the wild as he checked his coordinates.

Mingling with the wind, the voices howled in his ears.

"You're so ugly. So stupid."

"I'm going to lock you outside and feed you to the wolves!"

The voice of Bernadine Jordan floated through the air. Dolan glanced around him, but of course, there was no one there.

Only him and the shadows.

Bernadine was always with him, but now she was in his outer world, and he knew it was only a matter of time before she was with him in his inner world again.

And then the final stage of his plan would begin.

The sounds of every murder he'd committed wrapped around him. The wind was getting up and there were dark clouds in the sky. It was as if the earth was joining in the sadistic game of revenge that he was playing.

He forged ahead, heading for the final off-road point, realizing that his heart was racing at the thought of what lay ahead.

It seemed unbelievable, impossible, that his revenge was nearing completion.

The proof that he had completed his mission would be in her screams and her death.

Then he would be free.

The last leg of his journey was shorter than he'd expected. He skirted a couple of small cabins, and then drove around the lake, the snowmobile gobbling up the few remaining miles at high speed. He was riding into the setting sun, and it was getting dark when he finally saw it ahead.

There it was, just as his cellmate had described. A solid cabin, built to withstand ice and blizzards, rain and frost. A wind turbine outside, humming fast in the gale.

"Here I am," he said under his breath. "Are you ready for me yet, Bernadine? You're going to be very sorry for what you did."

He remembered the fear he had felt when she'd taunted him, and how her scathing comments, her scorn, her viciousness, had made him feel as if he was bleeding inside.

But now, his stomach tightened with tense excitement, because the time had come.

Dolan killed the ignition and waited to see if anyone came out of the cabin to investigate.

There was no sound except the howling of the wind.

Looking closer, he saw faint footprints leading away from the cabin's door. So she'd gone out somewhere. It was nearly dark and that must mean she would be back soon.

He didn't want his own footprints to clue her in. He could see a heavy door around the side of the cabin, leading to a separate room which was no doubt for storing goods and equipment.

Dolan drove the snowmobile to the back of the cabin where she wouldn't see it. It would be better to go in that way.

Knowing it would be dark inside, he took the flashlight from the snowmobile's storage compartment to help him navigate.

He switched on the flashlight and made his way toward the door, slipping and sliding and struggling against the strong wind.

Pushing open the door, Dolan saw it was pitch black inside. The flashlight's beam was steady and strong. It revealed stacked food, supplies, equipment. Coal and chopped wood. Oil and gas. He walked slowly through, gazing around at the new life she'd created for herself. Rope. Twine. There were many items here that would be useful, he decided with a smile.

The adjoining door to the cabin was closed. He put his shoulder to the door, and it gave way with a creak.

He was in. At last, he'd reached her room, where she lived and slept and dreamed. Briefly, Dolan wondered if she'd dreamed of him as often as he dreamed of her.

He shone the flashlight around the room, letting it show him the hiding place of his tormentor. His enemy. Her cruel, laughing face was imprinted on his mind.

It wasn't much better than prison, he thought with a callous laugh. In fact, it was a lot worse. This small, freezing cold room was stark and basic.

There was a small table and two chairs. A narrow cupboard. A single bed by the window. In the fireplace, a few logs smoldered, giving the room a smoky smell. That was another clue she had left recently and would return any minute, he decided.

He walked to the tiny window and looked out through the smeared glass. He could see nothing but the white wilderness beyond, and the frozen edge of the lake.

Dolan pulled out a chair and sat down on its hard, uncomfortable seat to wait, smiling as he looked around the cold, basic prison she had made for herself. He was thinking about the plans he'd put into place now, and afterward. He had a few more surprises up his sleeve that he would prepare after she arrived, in case any other unwanted visitors came by.

*

Half an hour later, he heard the footsteps he'd been waiting for.

The cabin door opened, and there she was. He had a moment to observe her as she walked inside. She was breathing hard, as if she'd been running. She wore a heavy, fur-lined parka. Her cheeks were flushed.

She was as tall and thin as he remembered. Those sharp cheekbones looked more pronounced. There were lines on her face that hadn't been there the last time he'd seen her. He remembered that after she'd taunted and bullied him, her face had snapped out of its ugly expression, straight back to beautiful, velvet smoothness.

He remembered her manicured hands and how those strong fingers could scratch and pinch. The perfume she had sprayed on her skin and the lipstick she'd worn. The way the heeled shoes had clicked as she strutted in her designer clothes.

But now there was no make-up, no perfume.

Now, in the hardness of her face, the coarseness of her skin, he saw the years had aged her and he had a sudden glimpse of what she would look like in a few decades, when time had further eaten away at her youthful beauty. At the same time, the knowledge amused him that she would never make it that far. She had only a few more hours of life to go.

And then she saw him quietly sitting there, and her face changed, tensing in fear.

She stood stock-still, staring at him as if he were a ghost. She gasped shakily.

"No," she stammered. "N-no."

"So you remember me," he said. "And you still recognize me. I'm touched, Bernadine."

"This - this can't be," she whispered. She'd turned pale as a sheet.

"I'm your worst nightmare. I'm the person you treated so badly all those years ago. I'm the person you laughed at and tormented. You have to pay for what you did to me. You're going to pay."

"I'm not!" she burst out. "You're wrong! It was never like that! Sure, I bullied you, but that was just older sister stuff. You were the evil one. I saw who you were. I was scared of you!"

Bernadine closed her mouth and he saw the direction of her eyes. He knew what she was going to do.

She was going to try and run. That amused him mightily. This silly girl honestly thought she was still bigger, taller, and faster than he was?

He got her even before she pushed the door open.

Grabbing her arm, he twisted his fingers into her flesh, knowing she would feel them painfully grinding against her bones. She tried to pull away and he allowed her to take in his strength. Those months of pushups in solitary were paying off. He didn't move as she struggled. Didn't even shift.

She stared at him, her mouth working, but no sound came out. Her eyes held a growing panic, the knowledge that she was in the clutches of a far more powerful and far more evil person than she could ever be.

He let his presence surround her, his eyes predatory and glittering. "You're going to pay," he said in a low, hypnotic voice. "For everything you've ever done to me. Every filthy little thing you've ever said. I'm going to make you feel the pain I felt."

He began to laugh. He wasn't sure why. It just bubbled up from him, and he couldn't stop. He felt the strength of his body as he picked her up and threw her down on the bed.

Then, he took out the ropes he'd brought through from the storeroom.

"We're going to have some fun for a while," he said, grabbing her wrists and reminding himself to make sure the knots were pulled as tight as they would go.

CHAPTER THIRTY

Missisa Lake. Missisa Lake. The words felt seared in Katie's mind as the SUV rushed down the deserted road, the strip of tarmac threading its way through the icy terrain.

She'd had a look on the map, and it was a large lake. It covered many miles. This was going to be a difficult hunt.

Her mind was racing, trying to work out where she should head. She only had a vague idea of what the cabin might be like.

Katie's only hope was that the locals might somehow know. When she got close to the lake, she was going to stop at a nearby fishing settlement, or cabin, if she could find such a place. In this faraway and inhospitable area, neighbors might be scarce, but she hoped that perhaps people would know who was who.

Just let her be alive, she prayed. He'd had many hours' lead on her.

Katie could see the lake ahead of her. The road was terrible. The SUV bumped and juddered as she rode toward it. It was a huge, frozen expanse of water.

"We're close, we're close," she muttered, her heart in her mouth.

She saw a tiny cabin near the south shore. Was this her cabin? Katie stopped and climbed out. The air stung her lungs. Ahead of her, swathed in furs, was a man fishing on the ice.

"Hello?" she called.

He turned to look, his face surprised and then distrustful as he saw her. A stranger in this village was highly unusual. She was sure almost nobody drove out this way.

The man watched her approach. He was short and stout, with a big wild bush of beard and hair.

He had a set of furs wrapped around him over his parka. A large tackle box stood a short distance from him.

"Can I help you?" he asked, his voice low and rather gruff.

"I'm looking for someone," Katie said.

The man said nothing, simply stood there, his face etched with distrust.

"A woman called Bernadine?" she added. In case he didn't know her name, she added, "The woman who stays in a cabin on her own. She's tall. With dark hair. Do you know where she lives?"

She saw his surprise. His brown eyes looked at her keenly. "What do you want her for?" he asked.

Katie decided on the truth.

"I want to warn her. She might be in danger. A killer has escaped from jail and he's looking for her." She showed her badge.

The man's face changed. He stood for a long, thoughtful moment.

"I think you might be too late," he said finally, and Katie's heart froze.

"What do you mean?" she said.

"Someone already drove that way. I saw a snowmobile heading around the lake, about an hour ago. It's only her cabin out there, about four miles further on."

"No," Katie whispered, horrified. Bernadine might be dead by now. She had to get to the cabin. Her mind recoiled from what he might already have done.

"Thank you," she said. "Thank you." She turned back to the SUV, but his shout stopped her.

"Wait a minute," he said. "You think she's really in danger?"

"I know she is," Katie said, feeling anguished that she hadn't gotten here earlier.

"Then don't go that way. Take the shortcut through the woods. It's faster. Go that way, and you'll be there in five minutes."

The man pointed to a faint track bordering the lake.

"Thank you." Katie ran back to her car.

She turned onto the lakeside. She realized that she'd have to drive slowly down here, as the track was treacherously uneven. But it was shorter than the road, which veered away from the lake to follow a route around the hillside.

Let me get there before he does, she prayed again and again, gripping the wheel as she drove.

The track led her through some thick woods. Stones scraped the undercarriage and branches whipped across the windshield. Then she reached a clearing and skirted the lake again.

And there it was, ahead of her. A small but solid wooden cabin. She had time to think how stark, lonely, and isolated it was. It was a weird place for an ex-model to hole up. There seemed to be little of life's comforts possible in this small, basic building set in such inhospitable surroundings.

As she roared up to it as fast as she could go, Katie wondered about Bernadine's mindset when she'd chosen this harsh, lonely life for herself. Had she regretted taunting Dolan? Or was it also that she'd wanted to turn her back on the materialistic world she'd occupied?

At any rate, this place felt like punishment.

She climbed out of the car. The wind was howling so strongly that it was distressing the snowdrifts. But in spite of the blowing snow, she could make out two faint sets of footprints from her vantage point. One leading to the door. One leading around the back.

She was too late. Dolan was inside.

Or was he?

Katie walked around the back. Where was his vehicle?

There it was. Her heart sank as she saw the red snowmobile that was hidden all the way at the back of the cabin. She walked over to it. It was cold. That meant he'd been there a while.

The wind must be too loud for him to have heard her through the cabin's thick walls. So she would have to go for speed and surprise, she decided, rushing around to the front of the cabin again.

There, she saw the door was open a crack. As she neared it, her blood was chilled by a high, terrified scream from inside.

Drawing her gun, she tiptoed to the door and looked through the gap.

Adrenaline surging, Katie took in her surroundings. Basic furnishings, cold and stark. A small bed. Bernadine was on it, tied to it. Her face was already bloody. Dolan had cut her cheeks, slicing deeply with a knife.

And there he was, the man she'd hunted remorselessly. He held a knife in his right hand.

Deciding to attack him as fast as she could, Katie shoved the door open, but as she did, from above her, she heard a ripping, groaning sound.

She had just enough time to think: he prepared. He booby trapped the door.

And then she dove to the side as the heavy logs he'd balanced above it came crashing down. One of them hit her shoulder, and pain lanced through her right arm.

Before she could get her balance, he was on her. He grabbed her right hand. Ripped her gun out of it. He was insanely strong. He had a deathly look of madness in his eyes.

Katie lashed out with her left fist. She caught him in the neck, and he grunted, but his grip did not loosen.

She tried to wriggle away from him, but he was too strong. He was breathing in desperate gasps, his eyes wild and mad.

"You bitch," he growled. Then he raised his knife and drove it down towards her.

She kicked as hard as she could, using all her power, hoping to fling the man off her before the knife could land. He was caught off balance and staggered back. Her eyes were on that knife. Its wicked blade was already stained with blood.

He tried again to get hold of her, but she held him off with her left hand, pushing and kicking and gouging with her fingernails. She knew she was fighting for her life. He would not hesitate to kill her. Fast. Because she was in his way and preventing him from finishing what he'd started.

From the bed, she heard Bernadine scream.

"Help! Help me!"

Katie wished she could. Right now, she was just trying to stay alive, with a shoulder on fire, and without a gun.

Dolan had clearly decided to go for a quicker way. With a flick of his wrist, he dropped the knife and grabbed her neck.

He wrapped his hands around it in a deadly stranglehold and fear lanced through Katie as she remembered the brutal, efficient way he'd killed. She had only seconds left.

She struggled as hard as she could, choking and gasping, doing her best to dislodge him. But with all his weight bearing down on her, she couldn't fight hard enough.

In another few moments, Katie knew, she would die, and leave Bernadine in the killer's clutches.

CHAPTER THIRTY ONE

The snowmobile bounced and skidded under Leblanc as he followed the icy, slippery road. At the small village earlier, he'd seen a fisherman on the ice, looking at him curiously. But, with faint tracks veering down to the lake, there had been no need to stop and ask the way.

He'd taken the chance. He'd swung off the main road and headed for the lake, in the hope they followed a shortcut leading to the cabin.

And then he'd seen the tracks, winding through the forest. He'd known then he was on the right path to the cabin. And now he was within sight of it.

Leblanc had been meeting with the search team north of Iroquois Falls when Katie's message had come through. Seeing where she was headed, he'd accepted the offer of a snowmobile to race north, thinking that if Dolan had chosen it as the quickest mode of transport, he would do the same.

Now, ahead, he finally saw the destination he needed. A small but solid, well-built log cabin.

Leblanc had no idea if he was in time. His bruised ankle was killing him. Pain was shooting up his leg and he could barely put weight on the limb, but now was not the time to allow an injury to slow him down.

He could see snowmobile tracks leading up to the cabin. He could see the tracks Katie's vehicle had left when she'd driven up. And there was her car. Some distance away.

But where was she?

He cut the engine and jumped off. Holding his gun, he rushed toward the cabin at a limping run. As he got there, he realized the door was partway open. But it was blocked by a pile of fallen logs.

He peered past them, aware of their strange, chemical smell as he stared inside. Then, he gasped in horror as he saw Katie on the floor, struggling with Dolan. He had his hands wrapped around her neck.

Leblanc's heart accelerated as he heard a scream from the bed in the corner where another woman, her face cut and bloody, was writhing to free herself.

Now feeling panicked, Leblanc triaged the situation. He couldn't get a clear shot at the guy. But right now, a shot would help. He needed to buy time. A bullet traveled faster than he could run.

He raised the gun and fired.

The shot blasted into the wall beside Dolan's head. The guy's head jerked up, his eyes wandering. He turned and saw Leblanc, and he flinched.

That moment gave Katie what she needed, Leblanc saw. His grip on her neck loosened, and she managed to head butt him in the chin.

Dolan reeled back. He lost his hold on her and that momentary pause gave Katie time to scramble out of reach, coughing and gasping.

Immediately, Leblanc fired again, hitting Dolan in the leg.

He went down, yelling in pain, clutching at his leg. Leblanc aimed again, stepping inside and over the logs. One more shot, and he would take him down.

But he wasn't just clutching at his leg, Leblanc saw, horrified. He was taking something out of his pocket.

Suddenly, the raw stink in the cabin made sense, as Dolan produced a lighter from his pocket.

With a flick of his fingers, he set the flame flickering. Then he lowered it, and the fire rushed along the line of gasoline he must have laid.

Leblanc stared at the flames in horror as they reached the pile of logs at the front door and roared into life. That way out was totally blocked.

Leaping away from the fire, he sprawled on the cabin floor. Looking up, he saw the cabin's back door slam shut. Dolan had disappeared through it, leaving them in this burning building.

Heat shimmered from the conflagration. He must have soaked the logs in gasoline. This cabin was ablaze, and Bernadine was tied to the bed, a prisoner in the room, yelling in terror.

"We have to save her!" Katie shouted, rushing over to the trapped woman and tugging at the knots that held her in place.

"We have to find a way out!" Leblanc limped to the back door. He flung himself against it.

It wouldn't open. Dolan must have locked it from the outside, but he was trapped in a burning room, and this was the only way out because the front door was now a conflagration. He had one chance. The heat from the flames was blistering. Choking smoke was flooding the cabin.

Leblanc rushed the door again. Gritting his teeth against the pain, he slammed his feet against it as hard as he could.

The door burst open, timber splintering from the latch.

Gasping in agony, he turned back, to see Katie was choking on the fumes, trying to untie the woman. Leblanc staggered back to help her, pulling at the knots. The woman was screaming hysterically. Smoke was blinding Leblanc as the knot finally came loose.

He grabbed Bernadine's arms and dragged her off the bed, hoping she could walk. She couldn't. She dropped to the ground, sobbing, and he had to drag her toward the door with him. The fire was swirling around their feet. It was a roaring, blistering inferno.

Holding his breath, Leblanc dragged her through the smoke-filled storeroom, with his leg buckling under him, and out into the snow. Gratefully, he dragged in a gasp of freezing air.

"Are you okay?" he asked Bernadine.

"I – I'm okay," she coughed. "He cut my face. He didn't hurt me otherwise. He threatened to."

Now, Leblanc needed to check on Katie.

He turned, looking for her. Then he stared at the cabin, panic filling him. He thought she'd been able to get out at the same time as him, before this horrendous fire had taken hold. But she hadn't made it out.

The cabin was now ablaze. Flames roared from the roof. But there was only one decision Leblanc could make. As fast as he could, he limped back to the open door.

CHAPTER THIRTY TWO

Katie choked on the smoke. Her eyes were burning, blinded. She couldn't believe that in this small cabin, she could not find the doorway, but the smoke was too thick. It was dark and suffocating and she couldn't see. She thought she heard screaming voices among the roaring flames, and imagined for a moment she heard Josie's voice, crying out inside her oxygen-starved mind.

Her hands were trembling as she reached around, and she felt splinters on the walls. Her fingers grazed over something, and she grabbed it, hoping it was the door, but it wasn't. It was scalding, molten hot and she snatched her hand away.

Tears streamed from her eyes as she tried to find a way out.

She could hear herself coughing as the smoke invaded her already damaged throat. She wanted to cry out, but she couldn't take a breath. If only she knew where to go, but the fire was everywhere, and the building was starting to collapse around her. The wall was leaning in, and a flaming beam crashed down, sending a shower of sparks up into the blaze.

She pushed herself away. Where was the doorway? It must be the other way. Backing toward the wall, she hoped she was going in the right direction. But the heat was intense, and her eyes were blurring.

And then a hand grabbed hers. She was dragged out. She was on the snow. The air above her was clear. Apart from Leblanc's concerned face, staring down at her. Choking, coughing, she managed to splutter out the words.

"I'm okay. I'm okay."

The chill of the snow had never felt so good after the inferno inside. The cabin was erupting in flames. Something exploded inside, with a dull booming, and the flames shot higher.

Katie struggled into a kneeling position and then she stood, gasping for breath, rubbing her shoulder.

She surveyed the scene.

Bernadine was sitting, hunched over in the snow, wrapping her jacket around her. She was cut and hurt and traumatized, but she was at least alive.

"We need to go after Dolan," Katie said.

Leblanc was staring at her, anguished.

"You're okay. That's the main thing. That's all that matters, really. But he will have too much of a head start on us. We won't catch him, now. We'll have to restart the hunt. Even our radio is gone. I still have my phone on me, I think." He groped inside his coat pocket.

"What do you mean?" Katie asked.

"He'll be at least ten minutes away on the snowmobile, going cross-country. And we can't follow." Leblanc stared at the place where he'd parked his vehicle. It was now consumed by flames.

"I don't think so." Smearing dust and soot from her face, Katie dug in her pocket. She took out a small silver key.

"He's not the only one who can set traps," she told him in satisfaction. "Before I went into the cabin, I took his snowmobile key."

Leblanc's dirty face split in a huge grin. "Well!" he said. "Then we need to track him."

Walking away from the cabin, Katie stared down at the scuffed snow.

"He went this way," she said, coughing again. "I can see the footprints. He went out to the lake. You stay here with Bernadine. I'll go and find him."

The tracks were easy to follow. Dolan had tried to cover them up with snow, but he'd done it hurriedly and the path was still clear. She headed out to the lake and saw him.

Dolan was lurching clumsily over the ice. He was leaving a thin trail of blood behind from the wound in his leg. She rushed onto the frozen surface in pursuit.

"Dolan!" she yelled, hoping he would stop, so that she could get a sight on him and shoot.

Dolan paused, staring back, fear in his eyes. But then he turned and started to run again.

Katie stepped out on the ice. But to her horror, she realized she couldn't follow.

She'd had years and years of walking on ice. She knew its moods. And this ice was unstable. There must be a warm current under it. It felt fractured, where water had moved underneath. It wouldn't hold.

But she had to get closer, to try for a shot.

Carefully, easing from foot to foot, she headed out on the treacherous surface.

Katie moved in total silence. She had learned this skill to perfection. The ice, she knew, was fragile. It had a life of its own. Moving forward carefully, she did not disturb it.

But Dolan didn't know its moods and he was running for his life. Katie could hear the crackling as he powered forward.

She watched as part of the ice cracked, alongside his tracks. Dolan fell, sprawling onto the ice. He was on his feet again. As he started to stumble forward again, the ice cracked and splintered once more. He had fallen into a hidden fissure.

She could feel the ice shivering.

She turned and threw herself backward, getting out of the danger zone as fast as she could. But Dolan was still running, clumsily, recklessly.

There was a long, eerie groaning. The split appeared, dark in the whiteness.

The ice was giving way. It was too late for Dolan. He was already in the middle of the fracture. He shifted from one foot to the other, the ice cracking under him, but he was too heavy to save himself.

With a horrified cry, he disappeared into the water. The ice closed over the sound of his screams.

Katie stared at the ice. There was no movement. No way of pulling him out. The lake had taken him.

He was gone.

CHAPTER THIRTY THREE

The rescue chopper soared into the air. Inside, Katie leaned back in the seat. Though noisy, it was warm, and the seat was plush and comfortable.

Bernadine was on a stretcher in the front, being attended to by a medic. The chopper was heading straight for a hospital where she would receive emergency treatment for her wounds and trauma.

The search party hadn't yet uncovered Dolan's body, but Katie was sure he must be dead. Nobody could survive under those icy waters for more than a few moments – or so she hoped.

Turning to Leblanc, Katie saw he looked as if he was deep in thought.

"What are you thinking?" she asked him.

"Bernadine wouldn't be here if it hadn't been for you. You saved her life," he said.

Katie shrugged. "Neither of us would be here if you hadn't arrived. I'm amazed you figured out where it was, using a totally different approach."

"Just as well," Leblanc grinned. His face was still dirty and soot-streaked, and his teeth looked even whiter in it.

Katie took another sip of her water, cold and refreshing, and passed the bottle to Leblanc.

It was time for her to say what she needed to him.

"I'm sorry," she said. "I didn't tell you the truth."

He nodded. "I knew you were hiding something. I didn't know what. I was angry and I overreacted."

"In Northfields, I spoke to the killer who I suspect murdered my twin." Katie took a deep breath. "I know you said you researched the story. But you wouldn't have known that it was my fault. I was the one who insisted we go out in bad weather. My parents rightly blamed me for it."

She couldn't look at him. Didn't want to see the sympathy in his eyes. Or worse still, the judgment.

"Everton denied having seen her. Most people believed she drowned. But I always knew in my heart that he took her. Of course, he would. But when I went and spoke to him in prison, he said she was the one he'd spared. That he never killed her."

Now she dared to look at Leblanc.

"What?" Leblanc looked stunned. "She was the one he spared? What do you make of that?"

She shook her head. "I have no idea. He could just be taunting me. I think it was a waste of time to go and speak to him. And it was the wrong thing to do. I should at least have told you. I feel terrible that I didn't."

She looked at him and saw he was shaking his head sadly.

"I am also to blame," Leblanc said. "I should have supported your decision to go, because it turned out to be correct. Dolan did go back to his old hunting ground. And, in fact, the information you got down there in the cells was what allowed me to reach you back there. I put you in a very difficult position by opposing you. And I've also been withholding facts that you have a right to know," he said awkwardly.

Katie felt startled as she looked at him.

"My case partner was killed, back in Paris. She was speaking to a jailed suspect, and there was a riot and prisoners escaped. I should have been there, and I wasn't. I will always blame myself for that."

Katie looked at him closely. From Leblanc's expression and the way he was speaking, she suspected that this person had been more than just a work colleague. Emotion filled his voice.

"I'm sorry," she said. "Thank you for telling me. I understand how painful that must have been. Don't blame yourself."

He shook his head. "I always will. If only we could turn time back, what different choices we would make." He paused. "You can't turn time back, but do you want to reopen your sister's case? Reinvestigate? I know it's been a long time, but sometimes information that's hidden at the time, is available later. If you want to do that, I will help you."

Katie stared at him, feeling filled with gratitude and something else, too. Hope.

"I'll think about it. That might be a good idea. Thanks, Leblanc."

She felt suddenly much lighter, as if a weight she hadn't known she was carrying had been lifted away. She decided she would do what Leblanc had suggested. Reopen the case. See if there was anything new to find.

But before she could do that, Katie knew there was something else that needed to be done.

*

Two days later, she walked up to the small wooden home that she hadn't seen for nearly fourteen years. Nerves bubbled inside her. She felt sick with dread and the memories were overwhelming her.

She paused at the gate and stared hard at the place where she'd grown up. Snow glittered in the grass and the sky was blue and clear. She could hear the river nearby, rushing and gurgling under the ice. That low roof was where she and Josie had jumped off, pretending to fly, landing in the deep, cold snow and laughing. That window was where she'd looked out, waiting for her father to walk up to the house from the shed where his boats were kept.

The place looked so peaceful. So quiet. So normal. Katie knew she had stayed away too long. She should never have been so scared to try. Mending things was difficult, but if you didn't try, old wounds festered. She had no idea what would happen. It might be a disaster. They might refuse to speak to her. But she had to try to heal the rift between herself and her parents.

The thought of facing them again felt hard and scary. Hesitating, she was suddenly not sure she could do this.

But she had to.

Taking a deep breath, she knocked on the door.

NOW AVAILABLE!

HIDE ME
(A Katie Winter FBI Suspense Thriller —Book 3)

When cross country skiers discover a body on the remote grounds of a luxury resort in northern Montana, FBI Special Agent Katie Winter must team up with her Canadian counterpart to stop a new serial killer before he strikes again.

"Molly Black has written a taut thriller that will keep you on the edge of your seat... I absolutely loved this book and can't wait to read the next book in the series!"
—Reader review for Girl One: Murder

HIDE ME is book #3 in a new series by #1 bestselling mystery and suspense author Molly Black.

FBI Special Agent Katie Winter is no stranger to frigid winters, isolation, and dangerous cases. With her sterling record of hunting down serial killers, she is a fast-rising star in the BAU, and Katie is the natural choice to partner with Canadian law enforcement to track the killer across the brutal and unforgiving landscape.

Yet Katie, lost in the secrets of her past, has finally found a lead into her missing sister—and this time she will track it down—even if she must battle a killer while doing so.

Can Katie keep it together long enough to solve both crimes?

Or will this case lead to her undoing?

A complex psychological crime thriller full of twists and turns and packed with heart-pounding suspense, the KATIE WINTER mystery series will make you fall in love with a brilliant new female protagonist and keep you turning pages late into the night.

Future books in the series will be available soon.

Molly Black

Bestselling author Molly Black is author of the MAYA GRAY FBI suspense thriller series, comprising nine books (and counting); the RYLIE WOLF FBI suspense thriller series, comprising six books (and counting); of the TAYLOR SAGE FBI suspense thriller series, comprising three books (and counting); and of the KATIE WINTER FBI suspense thriller series, comprising six books (and counting).

An avid reader and lifelong fan of the mystery and thriller genres, Molly loves to hear from you, so please feel free to visit www.mollyblackauthor.com to learn more and stay in touch.

BOOKS BY MOLLY BLACK

MAYA GRAY MYSTERY SERIES
GIRL ONE: MURDER (Book #1)
GIRL TWO: TAKEN (Book #2)
GIRL THREE: TRAPPED (Book #3)
GIRL FOUR: LURED (Book #4)
GIRL FIVE: BOUND (Book #5)
GIRL SIX: FORSAKEN (Book #6)
GIRL SEVEN: CRAVED (Book #7)
GIRL EIGHT: HUNTED (Book #8)
GIRL NINE: GONE (Book #9)

RYLIE WOLF FBI SUSPENSE THRILLER
FOUND YOU (Book #1)
CAUGHT YOU (Book #2)
SEE YOU (Book #3)
WANT YOU (Book #4)
TAKE YOU (Book #5)
DARE YOU (Book #6)

TAYLOR SAGE FBI SUSPENSE THRILLER
DON'T LOOK (Book #1)
DON'T BREATHE (Book #2)
DON'T RUN (Book #3)

KATIE WINTER FBI SUSPENSE THRILLER
SAVE ME (Book #1)
REACH ME (Book #2)
HIDE ME (Book #3)
BELIEVE ME (Book #4)
HELP ME (Book #5)
FORGET ME (Book #6)

CPSIA information can be obtained
at www.ICGtesting.com
Printed in the USA
LVHW041348071222
734739LV00002B/40